D0842549

Ace and Christi Series

The Red Rag Riddle

by
Grace Whitehart

Illustrated by
John Truman

SCHOOL OF TOMORROW®

Lewisville, Texas

SCHOOL OF TOMORROW
P.O. Box 299000
Lewisville, Texas 75029-9000

©1998 Accelerated Christian Education,® Inc.

ISBN 1-56265-056-4
3 4 5 Printing/Year 02 01
Printed in the United States of America

TABLE OF CONTENTS

CHAPTER 1

GOOSE BUMPS

It all started the day Ace had his scheduled checkup with Dr. Kindhart, the dentist.

Honk! H–o—n—k! Mrs. Virtueson blew the horn. Ace shook himself out of his daydreams, locked the back door of the house, and breathed in the sweet smell of early-summer flowers drifting over the driveway. The gentle June breeze that touched his light brown hair invited him to play outside. But he couldn't. He had something important to do first. He was going to the dentist. It wasn't exactly his idea of fun on such a lovely summer morning. No, he'd rather clean the garage or meet up with a grizzly bear. *Besides, I don't have a toothache*, he thought. It wasn't a matter of choice, however, so he silently climbed into the front seat of the car and buckled his seat belt. The spicy taste of cinnamon toothpaste still stung his lips, and the vinyl seats felt unusually stiff and uncomfortable. Maybe he was just imagining these things, though.

"You're not afraid to go to the dentist, are you?" his mother questioned. She didn't see him grimace as she backed out of the driveway. He **had** been brushing every day, but sometimes he did it in a hurry; and, well, sometimes he was simply too tired to floss.

"You can always buy new teeth like my grandmother's when you're older," Racer had suggested. The words echoed in Ace's ears and made him bite his lip. *What if I have to have a filling now? The dentist uses a drill for that, doesn't he?* Wh-r-r! The sound in his head made him shiver as prickly goose bumps popped up on his arm.

At the dentist's office, Ace sat down in the only remaining seat—a green, scratchy cloth sofa with hard buttons that jabbed into his legs. The whirring and slurping sounds coming from behind the closed door gave him more goose bumps. He could only imagine what the drill jabbing into his teeth

would feel like. *It isn't always good to have a keen imagination*, he concluded.

"Ace, the doctor is ready for you now."

Already? I just got here. Br-r-r. Ace felt a chill go up his neck. This visit wasn't getting any better. He walked into the examination room. There were the familiar funny-looking chair, strange metal equipment, and long, black curly cords and tubes. His nose twitched. The room smelled clean . . . like a hospital. Then he noticed them. On the white counter tops—lined up in a perfect row—tiny, sharp metal tools stared back at him. He knew for sure one of them must be a drill. Ace slowly climbed into the chair. The assistant briskly clipped the blue, stiff paper bib on him, tilted back the chair, and promptly began cleaning his teeth with gritty peppermint paste. *Yuck!* Ace immediately committed himself to proper tooth-brushing procedures.

When Dr. Kindhart stepped in, he extended his warm, brown hand. "Well, hello, young man," he said politely. He briefly glanced over Ace's chart. "It's been about a year since you were here last. Are you having any trouble with your teeth?"

"Not a bit, sir," Ace replied, hoping to make this visit as short as possible.

"Well, let's have a look anyway, just for fun."

I knew it. Ace's smile turned limp as he groaned inside. Dr. Kindhart moved the bright light until it shone on Ace's face.

"Okay, open wide." Ace's cold hands began to sweat. He closed his eyes tightly and opened his mouth as wide as he could. His jaws locked.

"Relax. I'm just going to check things out," Dr. Kindhart said. "Have you been brushing regularly?"

"Es, ur." The dentist's whole hand seemed to be in Ace's mouth.

"Good, good." Dr. Kindhart poked and picked. "Does this hurt?" Dr. Kindhart poked and picked a little more.

"No, ur," answered Ace, trying to swallow without choking. Saliva was pooling in his mouth.

"Suction, please," said Dr. Kindhart. His assistant stuck the suction tube into Ace's mouth and fished around a bit. It kind of tickled. Slup, slup, slup.

"How about this?" Dr. Kindhart continued as he picked at Ace's gums again.

"It urts uh iddle." Ace's cheek muscles ached.

Of course, it was hard for Ace to talk without closing his mouth, so Dr. Kindhart directed his questions to Mrs. Virtueson instead.

"How are things at Highland School? Is it out for the summer?"

"Y-e-e-s-s," Mrs. Virtueson sighed slowly. "We would really like to add computers to the Learning Center, but extra money is hard to come by right now," she said quietly.

"I understand," Dr. Kindhart nodded, moving to the other side of Ace's mouth. "Well, you can be sure that, if it's God's will, He will provide a way even if you can't see how right now."

It sounded as though Dr. Kindhart never doubted that God was always in control. After several more minutes, he finally clicked off the bright light. Ace slumped down like a wet noodle.

"Congratulations, Ace! I didn't find a single cavity."

"Whew!" Ace sighed on the outside. *Yip-e-e-e!* he shouted on the inside. Dr. Kindhart stepped on the pedal, and Ace's chair inched back up straight.

His checkup had not been so bad after all—not even the gritty peppermint paste. Ace ran his tongue over his teeth.

"Squeaky clean?" Dr. Kindhart winked. Ace laughed and slid off the chair to thank him, and soon he and his mother were off to the park to meet some friends.

Mrs. Virtueson told Ace she was pleased with his good report, but Ace was lost in thought. He didn't even hear her. *Computers for school. Wow! Our parents give us so much already. What can we do?* Suddenly, Ace's eyebrows shot up.

When the car stopped, Ace hopped out the door and ran across the grass. Shaking her head, Mrs. Virtueson smiled. *What has gotten into him?*

In the wooded park were parents, pets, and children. Ace looked around and soaked in the fresh smell of cedar and pine trees. Spotting his friends, Ace waved his hands and yelled, "Over here!" Hapford, Racer, Pudge, Reginald, Sandy, and Christi came running.

"What are you so excited about, Ace?" Racer asked breathlessly.

"Mother told Dr. Kindhart our school needs new computers, but there's no extra money right now." He paused and sucked in a deep breath before going on. "Wouldn't it be great if **we** could raise the money?" Stunned silence was the only reply.

"You mean w-work for it? On summer vacation?" Pudge stammered in disbelief. "You have to be kidding! Maybe I didn't clean out my ears well enough."

Sandy's hands flew to her hips. "Oh, come on, Pudge," she said. "I like Ace's idea. It's the least we can do. It might even be fun. But how can we do it?" she asked more thoughtfully.

"If I were old enough to baby-sit, I'd be glad to give any money I made this summer," said Christi.

"So would I." Sandy brushed her red bangs back out of her face.

"I know," Racer spoke up, trying to sound important. His eyes looked mischievous. "Maybe we can invent a scientific money-making machine with gears, switches, pulleys, and pipes with smoke coming out the top. I'm sure we could do it if we figured out how the levers . . ."

"Racer, if you were a cartoon character, you'd have a light bulb over your head in every frame," Hapford broke in.

"However, I think your money machine is against the law," Reginald observed. He swatted at a pesky gnat that tried to disguise itself among the freckles under his glasses. That accomplished, he continued, "Let's conduct a meeting and contemplate things we can do." Hapford wasn't sure exactly what that meant, but everyone listened because Reginald was so intelligent. The background yelling, barking, and squealing faded as the group moved farther away from the playground. They traipsed over and plopped down under a shady soapberry tree, while each waited for an idea to spring into his or her brain. Pudge twiddled his thumbs. Sandy stared at the clouds. Christi watched a ladybug climb a leaf.

"I have an idea," Happy suggested shyly. "Maybe we can have a lemonade stand or something. It gets really hot in the summer, so people get thirsty, and we have a lemon tree."

"Yeah," Racer agreed. "We can have a lemonade stand on Ace's busy street, and we can all work together. The boys can build the stand, and the girls can decorate it!"

"Now we're getting somewhere," Ace cheered. "If we keep thinking about it, I'm sure we can come up with even more things to do. Pastor Alltruth always says we should

do more than just pray. We should put 'feet' to our prayers—put action behind our words. God will help us find ways to make money, if we ask for His help and are ready to work hard."

Mrs. Virtueson glanced at them from a distance before turning back to the other mothers. *What are the children talking about so seriously?* she wondered.

No doubt the gray-suited stranger on a nearby bench wondered too. He peeked over the crumpled newspaper he was reading. With his big feet propped up on an old tree stump, his unmatched socks gave away his otherwise professional look. He folded the paper and hurriedly finished his sandwich, accidentally squirting mustard out the bottom. He sighed and pushed his thick glasses back up to the top of his broad nose. Then he wiped his mouth with a large, red handkerchief and forcefully scrubbed the fresh, yellow, gooey spot out of his black-and-white checkered tie until only a wet, yellow blotch remained. Finally, he placed his blue fedora squarely on his gray, balding head, stood up, and walked off. Nobody even gave him a second look . . . at the time.

CHAPTER 2

BASEBALLS AND BUBBLE GUM TRAILS

J. Michael sat curled up in the plump beanbag chair in the corner of his room. He loved to read. Now and then a pot or pan clanked noisily in the kitchen, until soon he smelled hot, fresh sweet potato pie baking in the oven. M-m-m . . . The scent of cinnamon and brown sugar drifted into every corner of his room. He could almost taste the soft, creamy pumpkin flavor in his mouth.

"J. Michael . . . time for supper!" J. Michael finished the sentence, slipped the marker into his book, and went to wash his hands. Walking down the hall, he overheard his father and stopped.

"Pudge's mother had a tooth filled this morning, and she said the Highland School students are doing special projects this summer to earn money for school computers. Isn't that something?"

"Of course!" J. Michael whispered, as he put his hand to his forehead. *Why didn't I think of that?* he wondered. *If Ace and his friends can work this summer to earn money for computers, why can't the students of Harmony School do the same? I'll check it out with Booker and Tom tomorrow.*

The next morning, when J. Michael, his father, Booker, Tom, and Joe arrived at the baseball field, the scent of wild flowers and leftover popcorn—from the game the night before—greeted them. Cleaning crews milled around with their pokers, picking up small bits of trash that the wind had blown into the fence and under the bleachers.

"Think fast, Booker." Tom threw a ball. Since moving into the neighborhood, Tom and Joe had become fast friends with Booker and J. Michael. They all loved the Lord . . . and baseball. They knew it didn't matter how they played baseball or how they looked, only who they really were on the inside.

"Hey, Tom," said Booker. "What has eighteen legs and catches flies?"

"I don't know. What?"

"A baseball team!" Booker giggled.

"Oh, really?" Tom came back. "Well, tell me. How can you keep cool at a baseball game?"

Booker paused and scratched his chin. "I give up," he shrugged. "How?"

"Stand next to a fan!" Tom laughed. Booker rolled his eyes and shook his head.

"Good one, Tom. Say, did you guys hear about the Little League game last night?" Booker tossed the ball back and forth from his bare hand to his smooth leather glove and cracked his bubble gum loudly. "The Patriots scored a home run in the bottom of the sixth inning! The ball rolled right to the edge of the fence!"

It was clear Booker thought nothing could be more exciting than baseball at the moment. J. Michael would just have to introduce his idea slowly.

Pitch. Ball! Pitch. Strike! Pitch. Hit! "All right!" Somehow between pitching and hitting and chasing the balls around, J. Michael managed to share the computer project idea with the other boys from Harmony.

"Sure, it may mean much work, but I believe we can earn enough money to buy a computer," Joe stated.

Booker stopped chewing his gum and pulled off his cap thoughtfully. "Yes. I think we can do it. Summer always seems long and boring when you don't have something special to do." He kicked up the dust around the pitcher's mound. "Even too much baseball can get old after a while, I suppose. I only hope we have enough time to make all the money we need to pay for a whole computer. How much does one cost, anyway?"

J. Michael pounded the dirt with his bat. "More than we have in our piggy banks, for sure," he answered.

While they talked, one of the part-time workers continued collecting old bits of hot dog, crushed cups, and peanut shells around the stands. Working on weekends was usually dull for him; but this morning he thought to himself, *Isn't this interesting? A second group of youngsters planning to help their school! We're talking about a lot of*

money! The man secretly listened to the boys and had an idea of his own. When what looked like a red rag fell out of his back pocket, he quickly stuffed it back in and continued gathering trash. As he moved around, his shoe stuck to a piece of fresh bubble gum on the pavement. With long, pink strings of bubble gum trailing from his shoe, how could the boys not notice him?

CHAPTER 3

READY OR NOT!

The air was dry, still, and quiet. Leaves hung motionless. The Virtuesons' pink petunias drooped, and their petals wilted as the stems bowed low to the ground. *Hm-pf-f. Lazy flowers*, Racer thought. *They're always in their beds.* Though it was only nine o'clock in the morning, it was already very hot. Racer lifted the bronze door knocker. "Ouch!" It burned his hand. He rang the doorbell instead.

Ding-dong. He shifted from one foot to the other and hoped he wouldn't melt before someone came to answer the door.

"I'll get it," Ace called inside. Today, he and Racer were going to figure out how to set up the lemonade stand.

Ace answered the door and both boys strolled into the kitchen, sat down, and tried to look as if they knew what they were doing. Neither of them had the first clue about running a business, however, so they just sat there.

"Let's see . . . What do we need to do first?" Ace drummed his fingers on the table and stared at the ceiling. Racer wrinkled his nose and stared at the floor.

"How about making a list of all the things you need?" hinted Mrs. Virtueson kindly.

"Good idea." Ace rolled up his sleeves and wrote WHAT WE NEED on his notebook paper. "First we need a place to set up the stand."

"I still think near the sidewalk out front would be a good place," Racer said decisively. "Many people go past on this street."

"It would make a fine location," Mrs. Virtueson agreed.

"And we'll need something to make a stand or a table," Racer said. "I know." He jumped up. "We have a wooden packing crate in our shed. We could nail some boards on it to make a real sturdy stand."

"And we'll make signs so people will know what we're doing," said Ace. "You know, if we already had a computer, we could use it to make some really neat signs."

"Yes, but we don't have a computer already." Racer slumped back into his chair. They thought some more. This time Ace looked at the floor and Racer looked at the ceiling.

"H-m-m," Ace muttered. "My dad has a computer at the church office; maybe he could help us make some good signs. I'll ask."

"Oh!" Racer exclaimed as a thought came. "A pitcher for the lemonade, and how about fliers to give to people who live around here?" Racer added.

"Yeah. We could make some fliers with colored markers," suggested Ace.

"Do you think we could really make that many?" Racer remarked as he started counting numbers in his head. "My hand hurts just thinking about it!"

"We can if we work hard. It might take several days, but we can do it," Ace insisted. "Well, it looks as if there's only one other thing . . . an ice chest to keep the lemonade cold," said Ace.

"I'll ask Dad and Mom if we may use our old one," Racer said.

"That's all then, I suppose," remarked Ace. He smiled and put down his pencil. "We did it! That was easier than I thought."

Mrs. Virtueson had been silent. Now she looked thoughtfully from one boy to the other. "Is that all you need?" she asked. She wanted to see if the boys were really thinking through every detail.

They looked at each other and then back at her.

"Don't you think you've forgotten a few things?" she pushed. They still looked blank. "What about lemons, sugar, ice, cups, a money box—and how you're going to pay for the things you need?"

Racer's eyes got very big. He put his head down on the table.

"I never dreamed a lemonade stand could be so much work," Ace groaned. He propped his elbows on the table and rested his chin in his hands. "Mom, can we really do this? Could you help us?"

"What if I give you the money you need to get started and you pay me back out of your profits?"

"Would you, Mom?"

"Of course," she nodded.

"You won't be sorry. We'll have the best lemonade stand in town."

"Now, before you get in too big a hurry, you need to make the fliers; then take care of the other things. No one will stop if they don't know about the sale."

"We should be able to open this stand by next Monday, don't you think?" Racer asked Ace, as they walked out of the kitchen.

Yes, Monday would be the Grand Opening.

*   *   *   *   *   *   *

In the next few days, both boys designed, printed, and colored their signs. Friday, Racer spent the night with Ace. They had made so many fliers that Racer dreamed

he was being chased in his pajamas by an army of colored markers as he ran wildly across long, endless sheets of white paper. Finally morning came. Birds chirped and twittered, lawn mowers cranked up, and children all over town began begging for breakfast . . . all children except Racer and Ace, that is.

The boys were supposed to set up the lemonade stand early that morning so Sandy and Christi could decorate it and tack up signs, but they were having a hard time of it. Racer rolled over and pulled the goose feather pillow over his head. He groaned. Still tired from his funny dream, he pretended it wasn't morning. Not until the noisy garbage truck squawked and signaled for trash, did Ace finally get up and start down the stairs. In a few minutes, Racer did follow—his nose begging his stomach along. He straggled into the kitchen in his pajamas, his jet-black hair sprouting out on all sides.

"M-m-m," he grinned. "Am I still dreaming, or is breakfast ready?"

"Am I also dreaming, or is that a new haircut?" Ace teased. Racer checked his reflection in the shiny metal toaster. Startled, he looked away.

"As a matter of fact," Racer played along, "I think it's called a flattop. You lie **flat** on the **top** of your pillow for a night, and when you wake up—ta-dah!"

Mrs. Virtueson laughed. "Have a seat, Racer. Your pancakes are coming up."

When the boys were ready to go, Mrs. Virtueson drove them to the store. Spotting the fruits and vegetables, they set about finding the items on their list. Ace and Racer stared at the piles and piles of colorful fruit—all different shapes and sizes. The lemons could come from Hapford's tree, but the limes would have to come from here. Okay . . . *How many limes does it take to make fresh-squeezed limeade?* Ace's mouth puckered as he imagined licking the juice off his fingers. He picked up one of the best-looking limes from the bottom of the pile. It smelled so good, but . . . Plop! Plop! "Uh-oh." He knew what was coming. His mother reached out, but it was too late. Bump-bump-bump-bump-bump! A tidal wave of limes rushed to the floor. Ace's face turned as red as a fire engine.

"W-W-W-Whoops!" A man accidentally backed into an overhead scale for weighing fruit and stepped on one of the slippery limes. The bump knocked his glasses to the floor. The pencil behind his ear fell down beside them. He felt around and by mistake picked up the wet, sticky piece of fruit instead. "Yuck!" he muttered before replacing his glasses properly on his nose. His eyes met Ace's. The man jumped back. He rushed off, wiping his sticky hands on a piece of red cloth. Ace thought the man looked somewhat familiar. But why? From where? *He isn't even carrying a basket or pushing a cart. And why does he seem frightened?* Ace wondered.

Forgetting the stranger, Racer poked Ace in the ribs. "Fresh-squeezed, huh?" he teased. "That's fine with me, but maybe we

should ask Hapford to plant a lime tree too. It might be less embarrassing."

"Racer, cut it out! Who was that man?"

"The one with the red rag?" asked Racer.

Ace nodded.

"Beats me. I don't know. I never saw him before."

"Are you sure?" Ace pressed. Racer nodded.

Meanwhile, as Mrs. Virtueson and the boys finished their shopping, Christi and Sandy helped Mr. Virtueson nail the last boards in place on the lemonade stand. Finally, it was all ready for the finishing touches. They hadn't told Ace and Racer that they were bringing along a few "extras" to make the stand look even more inviting. Christi had brought a few yards of long, white lace ruffle, which she fastened to the top and sides. Sandy had a bright blue checkered tablecloth and a white plastic vase for wildflowers. The girls were delighted. The freshly picked violets, dandelions, and daisies would surely attract more customers. They just knew it.

When the boys got home, the girls happily pulled them over to the stand. "What do you think?" asked Christi.

Racer pushed his lower jaw back in place after nearly dropping the grocery bag he carried. "I . . . um . . . well . . . uh . . . ." He was speechless.

"It's all ready for Monday! Don't you love it?" Sandy clapped her hands together, her eyes sparkling.

"Uh . . . yeah . . ." Racer finally said.

Ace was about to say something too, when . . .

Beep! Beep!

"Oh, my mom's here," announced Christi. "Sorry. We have to go! I have a piano lesson! Bye!" The girls grabbed their empty sacks and took off without another word.

Ace looked at Racer. Racer looked at Ace. They looked at the lemonade stand . . . the ruffles . . . the lace . . . the flowers. Racer rolled his big eyes. "Girls!" he moaned.

CHAPTER 4

A NOT-SO-BOOMING BUSINESS

"There!" Racer said as he squeezed out the last drop of lemon juice.

Ace picked out the seeds and poured the sour liquid into a plastic pitcher. "O-o-oh!" he exclaimed as he tasted it. His tongue almost curled into a knot. He added some scoops of sugar, more water, tasted again, and smacked his lips. "Perfect." Picking lemons from Hapford's tree was the best decision after all. They were fresh, ripe, and **free**.

Racer and Ace each carried out a pitcher, one of lemonade and one of limeade. It was Monday morning, and at last everything was ready for the "Grand Opening."

"Maybe we can make enough money in one day to buy a computer!" said Racer hopefully.

They waited and watched. No customers came. They rearranged the table and switched seats. Still, no customers came. "I'll go stand on the sidewalk with a sign,"

Racer offered. He paced up the sidewalk like a professional salesman. "Limeade! Get your ice-cold limeade here! Only fifty cents a cup!" Turning around, he paced back down the sidewalk, "Get your ice-cold lemonade here! You'll enjoy it! Only fifty cents a cup!" he called.

Thirty minutes later, his voice was scratchy and hoarse. "Hello-o-o-o," he called out. "Anybody home?" He looked like a tin man—eyes straight ahead, body stiff, mindlessly marching up and down. Finally, he dragged himself back to the lemonade stand. *It must be the ruffles.* He shook his head and sighed. Two more cars went by without stopping. Racer was discouraged.

"Look!" he suddenly shouted. His eyes lit up. "Here comes Miss Martha!" The boys sat up straight and smiled. But she crossed the street before reaching them. "Oh, Ace, let's give her a free lemonade—like a door prize or something. Miss Ma-ar-tha-a!" Racer called out without thinking.

She turned and looked up sourly. "You're not going to get one dime out of me, young man! You shouldn't even be asking an old woman like me for money. You ought to be ashamed of yourself," she remarked bitterly, stamping her cane on the smooth, hot sidewalk. The tight, white bun on top of her head didn't budge.

Racer quickly poured a cup of lemonade, anyway, and started over to her. She lifted her cane and shook it. "Not one step closer, you hear? I said I have nothing to give you. Don't you hear me?"

"Miss Martha, we want to give you this. We're not asking for money. Really, it's free." He held it out. "You're the first person to walk by, so we're giving you a surprise!" Racer said gleefully.

"Poison for all I know," she muttered. "Besides, I hate surprises." She stuck her nose in the air and proudly said, "I refuse to be given anything I haven't earned or haven't paid for myself. Now go away so I can get out of this heat, you terrible boy. Scoot. Scoot! Out of my way!" She waved her long wooden cane at him again.

Racer hung his head. *We can't even give the lemonade away. She doesn't even know how to be an old lady. Old ladies are supposed to knit, smile, bake you things, and tell you what a nice young man you are.*

Not even an ice-cold drink on a hot day could put Miss Martha in a good mood. She didn't want anything she couldn't earn or pay for herself! No wonder she rejected God's gift of eternal life.

A big cloud moved across the sky to offer a little welcome shade from the fierce summer sun. *"Ah-h! Finally!"* Racer murmured as the afternoon dragged on.

Ace glanced at his watch. The second hand moved so-o-o slowly. He shook the watch and held it to his ear. "That's it," he announced suddenly. "I'm thirsty. Let's drink a cup of lemonade."

Racer's parched throat made him nod eagerly. The boys drank down a big cupful apiece. Racer wiped his mouth with the back of his hand. After all, he **was** outside. They were still thirsty, though, so they each poured another cup. This time they had a cup of limeade.

Cr-r-rash!

"What was that?" shouted Racer.

"Hm-pf-f! It almost sounded like thunder," Ace chuckled.

Cr-r-rash! Plink! Plink! Plink! Plink!

Racer looked up in time to get hit in the eye with a big raindrop. "Agh!" he cried. "It **was** thunder!" The boys leaped out of their chairs and stumbled around gathering their things. Rain began to streak down their faces and felt like tiny pins pricking their bare arms. Boom! The sound of thunder rumbled toward them like a train. Mrs. Virtueson popped out the door.

"Hurry!" she called. "Get what you can." Each grabbed what he could carry and, tripping over each other, fell through the door.

Safely inside, Mrs. Virtueson tossed the boys some warm, fluffy towels from the clothes dryer. They peeled off their soggy socks and dried off as best they could. Zip! A bright orange flash of lightning tore across the black sky as if trying to split it in two. Looking out the window, Ace saw Sandy's vase topple over. The wind scattered the wildflowers freely. Christi's pretty lace looked more like old, crumpled rags than ruffles. The signs, too, were completely ruined.

Looking out the window, the boys never noticed a midnight blue car quietly start up near the Virtuesons' home. Its driver shook his head as he slowly rolled past the lemonade stand. Beating rain blinded his vision as the front tire accidentally brushed against the curb. The car splashed through deep puddles and fog crept onto the windshield. He resisted the urge to draw a picture and, instead, hastily wiped the moisture cloud with a bright red rag. Then he drove on.

Dark, puffy rain clouds remained close to the ground. Ace slumped in an overstuffed wing chair. *I wonder what causes thunderstorms. Where do they come from? Why did one have to come so quickly today?* he wondered. *They're mysterious*

sometimes. He frowned, and his eyes clouded over. His mind wandered to all the trouble they'd been having and the strange things that had been happening. Boom! Another crash of thunder shattered his thoughts.

"It's all my fault," Racer said leaning back and closing his eyes.

"What did you say, Racer?" Mrs. Virtueson asked.

"I said, 'It's all my fault.' I prayed God would make it cooler outside. Then the thunderstorm came. I guess I should be more careful when I pray."

Mrs. Virtueson chuckled. "Yes, Racer. We should be careful what we pray for—God just might give it to us in ways we don't expect!"

It was a l-o-n-g day. Even though Racer stayed for dinner, it was a quiet meal, which was most unusual. Neither boy felt much like talking. Racer pushed food around his plate while Ace stuck his fork in and out of his mashed potatoes. Neither boy felt much like eating.

After awhile, Mr. Virtueson cleared his throat and spoke up thoughtfully. "Many people aren't home on weekdays. Perhaps you should set up the lemonade stand on Saturdays. Almost everyone does yard work on weekends. People garden, trim hedges, or pull weeds—the kind of work that makes a person thirsty." Ace's face brightened.

"But we didn't even make a single cent today . . . not one penny!" moaned Racer. "I thought we could've paid for at least one computer today," Racer continued. "Is that too much to ask? At this rate, it's going to take **forever** to buy a computer."

"Your ambition is a good sign, Racer. If you two boys persevere, the profits will come," Mr. Virtueson encouraged. "With perseverance and God's blessing, they will come."

CHAPTER 5

A REAL DEAL

When the rays of the morning sun tiptoed through his window, Ace's eyes popped open. He yawned once and scrambled out of bed. Today was Saturday. He had waited all week for this day.

Hurrying through dressing and breakfast, he was finally ready to rush outside to the lemonade stand. Sandy and Christi had brought balloons this time instead of ruffles, and business was booming by lunchtime. Mr. Virtueson had been right. Most neighbors did spend Saturdays working outside. The whine of chain saws, lawn mowers, and trimmers filled the air. One young neighbor watered yellow and purple pansies along her front walk. Another tried to convince her curious two-year-old that the freshly mowed grass wouldn't taste good. An old man in loose-fitting overalls gathered radishes, lettuce, and spinach from his garden, while the little fellow beside him dug up pink worms that poked their heads

out of the rich, black earth. Something **was** different about Saturdays. In fact, business was so brisk, Mrs. Virtueson had to rush to the store after lunch to get more supplies.

By suppertime, only a small amount of each drink remained at the bottom of the pitchers. Now, this was what having a business was supposed to be like! As Mrs. Virtueson called Ace and Racer inside for a moment, the girls prepared to close the stand. Just then a man in navy blue work pants hurried up to the stand and peered into each pitcher.

"Oh," he frowned in disappointment, "there's not enough of either kind to fill a cup."

Christi frowned too and then laughed eagerly. "How about some punch? We'll just pour all the juice into one cup, and you can have it at half price."

"Now that's a real deal. Thanks." The man smiled and wiped his sweaty forehead with a red cotton bandanna. He took one big gulp and finished off the punch. "Ah-h! That hit the spot. Keep the change, and keep up the good work," he said. The man left a twenty-dollar bill and hurried away before the girls even noticed and could say, "Thank you!"

"**Who** was that?" Sandy asked in disbelief. They rushed inside to tell Ace and Racer.

"Who left all that?" Racer asked.

"What did he look like?" Ace interrupted.

"He was tall with gray hair and dark sunglasses," said Christi.

"And he had smudge marks on his chin," said Sandy. "But everyone gets dirty working outside on Saturdays. Why do you ask?" Sandy wanted to know.

"Oh, no special reason," Ace muttered. "Do you remember anything else?" he questioned.

Christi added slowly, "I do remember that he had a big bandanna stuffed in his shirt pocket. That seemed a little strange." Ace's heart beat faster.

"I think it was bright orange," said Sandy confidently. "O-o-or maybe hot pink . . ." she said, not so confidently.

Christi shook her head and shrugged. Neither of the girls had really been paying attention. They were just happy to make a profit for the computers!

It seemed to Ace that mysterious people were popping up in strange places, doing strange things. Well, at least one mysterious person anyway. He wasn't sure if he should tell his dad and mom yet. Racer and Ace gave each other puzzled looks about this "neighbor." Was it the man they had seen at the grocery store? Perhaps.

CHAPTER 6

KATIE SPRINGER'S KITTY AND THE SPY

"How did we happen to pick the hottest Friday of the year to have a yard sale?" asked Miriam. She tried, without success, to keep a pair of socks from tumbling over the edge of a more-than-full basket of clothes.

Tables had been set up in a large vacant lot at the edge of town; and before long, shoppers crowded around, pawing through this and that as they searched for bargains and treasures. Mr. Trueword and Reginald Upright totaled prices and collected money, while the parents and students of Harmony and Highland tried in vain to keep the tables neat.

Pudge, Happy, and J. Michael had tables side by side. Hapford's held a wide variety of toys—yo-yos, blocks, rubber balls, puzzles, model airplanes, and even a chemistry set with real chemicals and test tubes. Pudge and J. Michael manned a separate table. It contained a myriad of small electrical appliances—mixers, irons, toasters, saws, and drills.

"Does this drill work?" a skinny boy asked Pudge sourly. He looked about ten years old. His jeans were faded and torn, and his shirt was smudged with grease. A little leftover breakfast—grape jelly to be exact—stained one sleeve, which perhaps he had used as a napkin.

"Yes, it does work," replied Pudge eagerly. "We tried them before the sale."

"I see. The label says three dollars." The boy mumbled something under his breath. He carefully returned the drill to its box and slowly closed the lid. He waited a few seconds. Then he opened the lid again and touched the drill a second time. After a third time of opening and closing the lid, he put the box under his arm and reached into his pocket for some money. His dirty fingers felt around and wiggled out a hole in the bottom. Nothing. He reached in the other pocket and pulled out an old candy wrapper, a fishhook, a paper clip, a crumpled note, and some change. "Just a minute," he

murmured. "Here. How much is that? I'm not so good at math." He handed Pudge the money.

"Um-m. One dollar and eighty-one cents," Pudge counted.

"Aw-w . . . not enough, huh? Okay. Hold on a minute. I just gotta buy this for my dad. He needs a drill to fix up the house."

"Really? Where do you live?"

"Oh, just over there." He pointed vaguely over his shoulder. All Pudge and J. Michael saw was a rusty, old, beat-up bus parked at the edge of the lot.

"In that bus?" Pudge said, trying to hide his surprise.

The boy looked down. He blushed, but he quickly stuck his chin out and said, "Hey, it's cool. We travel all over the country without even leaving our house! Not very many kids can do that, 'cause they're in school all the time."

"Don't you go to school?" J. Michael wondered out loud.

"Naw. Who needs it? My pop didn't go to school, and look at him. Besides, he says too much studying fries the brain." He jerked his shoulders uncomfortably.

"What does your father do for a living?" Pudge tried to get more information.

"Hm-pf-f. He's his own boss. He gets to do whatever he wants. Usually he takes jobs out West picking grapefruit, apples, or peaches. Hey, ever had a peach-pit fight or an apple-seed-spittin' contest? You're missing a lot of fun if you haven't. We do stuff like that all the time. Ye-sir-e-e. We live an exciting life—never know where we'll be tomorrow or when we'll get to eat next. You know, like in a book or something . . ." Realizing he had said more than enough, he stopped. "Oh, sorry. I was looking for money now, wasn't I?"

The boy reached into his back pocket and pulled out a worn leather wallet. J. Michael could plainly see it had no money in it.

"Doesn't it get hot? I mean . . . it being summer and all." J. Michael motioned back toward the bus.

"Sure. The heat makes you tough. A real man can take it," the boy answered, trying to convince himself also.

"Do you have any brothers or sisters?"

"Oh, yes. There's me, Barry, Jimmy and Jack—they're twins—and Katie. Five in all. I'm the oldest. Bobby Springer is the name," he said, popping his suspenders and feeling important. "Listen, would you save this drill for me? Maybe I'll find some more money in the parking lot or down by the creek. I can find all sorts of treasures—like this fishing hook. Did you see it?" he grinned, showing a missing tooth.

"Yes. That'll be great when you go fishing," agreed J. Michael. "Say, let me have a look at that drill again." J. Michael pretended to look it over carefully. "You know . . . I think someone put the wrong price on this. It was only supposed to be marked one dollar and fifty cents." Pudge, who had been busy with another customer, raised an eyebrow; but J. Michael gave him a look to be quiet and changed the price on the tag.

"Oh, boy! A dollar fifty? Really? Wait'll my dad sees this! Now he can fix Mama's dresser . . . and the clock . . . and the shelves . . . and the front door!" He impatiently handed over the money, ready to lock his fingers around that drill. "Now I have to find my little sister, Katie, before Mama finds me first! It's time to eat, and I'm hungry." He ran off. Pudge and J. Michael noticed he was barefoot, but that wasn't necessarily so unusual on a hot summer day. Another customer came by, and no more was said about it.

When lunchtime came, the children took turns eating. Pudge had to loosen his belt one more notch. He brushed scraps of leftover sandwich meat and bread crumbs onto the ground. One boy threw an apple core over his shoulder into a patch of wild grass. Miriam peeled an orange over the trash can, but a few pieces missed the opening. No one knew a hungry mouth was behind the thick trees, waiting to scavenge every precious bite.

Everyone kept busy until late afternoon. "We really need to close the sale before it gets dark," said Mrs. Peace, folding the remaining clothes and placing them in a box.

The glowing sun began to set, and dusk lazily crept upon them. As fireflies blinked their secret messages, the only sounds were the chirping of crickets, the bellowing of bullfrogs, and the scuffing of box flaps as they were closed.

Soon only one table and two customers remained. One was a man wearing pleated black pants and an orange-and-purple striped shirt under a sport coat. The other was a small girl looking to be no more than four or five years old. She really didn't seem to be a shopper at all. She lovingly picked up a pink T-shirt with a fluffy, white lamb design on it. Sandy's little sister Becky smiled and watched. Her pigtails bounced up and down as she skipped over and asked, "Want to play?" The little girl stared down at the ground, embarrassed. Becky asked again. The girl still did not speak. Becky skipped back to her mother and tugged at her skirt. "That girl's funny. She doesn't want to play with me."

"Honey, she doesn't even know you," Mrs. McMercy said. "Wouldn't you be shy if you were surrounded by people you didn't know?"

"Oh, no. I'm not shy at such a big age," she answered. Mrs. Virtueson, who was nearby, smiled as she looked down at Becky—all of five years old.

Suddenly the other little girl saw something moving in the grass.

"Look at the sweet kitty," she squealed. "Come here, little kitty. I won't hurt you. Oh-h-h . . . You're so pretty. I've never seen a black kitty with a big white stripe down its back." She reached for it. The animal growled and stamped its front feet.

Sp-plish! Something wet flew through the air, hit her legs, and started dripping into her shoes.

"A-a-a-a-u-g-h-h-h!" The little girl screamed and dropped the shirt.

"Katie!" called a woman from the door of the old bus. The woman looked very tired. Her faded cotton housedress made her appear even more worn out. Her hair was tied up in a jumbled knot, with loose strands hanging around her face. *I already have enough problems*, she thought.

"Oh, Mommy, help me! Please, help me!" the little girl ran around in circles. Everyone's noses told them the "kitty" was a mother skunk, who had hoped to feast on a few of the tasty tidbits the students left from lunch.

"Phew! I've never smelled anything so bad." Sandy bent over and choked.

"Let's get out of here," Booker moaned, holding his baseball cap over his face. He would really have liked a gas mask, but his cap was the best thing he could come up with at the moment.

"Help me! Somebody help me," Katie cried, running toward the old bus.

Her mother stepped from the bus. "Oh, no, you don't. You can't go in there smelling like that," she declared and

slammed the bus door shut. She and Katie ran back to the parking lot, looking for anybody who would help them. Bobby was still down at the creek, so he didn't know what was going on.

Pudge walked as close to Katie as he dared and tried to comfort her. "You're going to be all right," he said, holding his nose. "You're Katie, aren't you? I recognize your 'house.' Come here; we'll get you cleaned up." The girl looked at him, unsure if she could trust him. The tears running down her cheeks were as much from the strong smell as from fright. "Don't worry!" Pudge choked. "My mother told me tomato juice will take out skunk smell, and somebody has already gone to get some."

"You mean all I have to do is drink it?" she asked, wiping her eyes.

"Something like that," Pudge explained.

The girl's mother watched as Pudge talked with Katie. His kindness puzzled her. She was glad he was trying to help her daughter, but she was unsure too.

What kind of people helped strangers? It was beyond her. As long as they helped and didn't hurt Katie, though, she would just watch. At least attention was off the bus house and why it was there. She hoped they wouldn't start asking too many questions.

Still holding her nose, Katie sobbed into Pudge's shirt. "I'm so sorry. I thought the kitty would like me. I guess it didn't. I dropped the shirt on it, but why did it spray stinky stuff on me?"

Before Pudge could answer, Dr. Kindhart came back. He opened a can of tomato juice, while Mrs. McMercy pulled Katie gently away from Pudge.

Katie's mother continued watching. She knew what they were doing and was grateful. She had no money to spend on tomato juice, but Katie was getting help. That was what mattered.

Katie's eyes were puffy and red. Her lower lip hung out. Mrs. McMercy wiped the sweaty strands of hair sticking to Katie's hot, flushed cheeks.

"Take a deep breath, honey." Katie did, and Dr. Kindhart started pouring the cool, thick juice over her head.

She wrinkled her nose and rubbed her arms. "Icky . . . icky." She didn't like the slippery feel of tomato juice running down and soaking her clothes.

"Is this how I'm s'posed to drink it?" she asked, looking at Pudge. He nodded and opened another can.

"Take off your tennis shoes, Katie. I don't think we can save them," Mrs. McMercy said sadly.

"No," Katie begged. "It's the only pair I have."

"We'll get you a new pair and some fresh clothes too," promised Mrs. McMercy.

Almost everyone had forgotten the other "customer" who still remained. He was hurriedly scribbling some notes. The way Pudge and the others handled the skunk incident didn't surprise him. Although he pretended to continue looking at merchandise, his gaze never really strayed from the activities of the students, the parents, and Katie—until his pen quit working. He shook it to see if it were empty. It still wouldn't write, so he gave it one last good shake. Ink bled all over his hands. Frustrated, he pulled a red, decorative scarf out of a pocket in his sport coat. *A sport coat on a hot summer day?* Ace noticed the scarf and remembered the man from the grocery store. As he started to walk over to ask him some questions, his mother asked him to carry a box to the car. He obeyed, and when he came back, the "customer" was gone. The man had made a quick exit. *Who is he anyway?* thought Ace. *A pickpocket? A thief? An outlaw?* Ace scolded himself for making too much of this. J. Michael and Booker hadn't mentioned one thing about any mysterious man. He was probably just a stranger who didn't mean any harm. Then again, maybe he was a spy!

CHAPTER 7

SNOWY'S IT!

"Catch, Sport!" J. Michael yelled. He threw a stick across the backyard. The dog chased after the stick as it sailed across the soft grass. He grabbed it and raced back to J. Michael. He plopped the stick on the grass and wagged his tail expectantly. J. Michael didn't even notice. His mind was on Bobby Springer and little Katie. How long had the Springers been living in Highland City? When would they move again? Did the children go hungry? How did they live in that bus? So many unanswered questions. *I'll talk with Pastor Gentle. I know he would want to know about them. Maybe he could even stop by for a visit.*

Unlike J. Michael, Sport **wasn't** thinking about the Springers; he spied J. Michael's shoelaces and growled at them. When they didn't growl back, Sport grabbed one string with his teeth and yanked.

Since the shoestrings didn't seem to be putting up a fight, he pulled even harder to start a game of tug of war.

"Silly dog." J. Michael dropped to his knees and stroked behind the dog's ears. *Lord, please show me how we can help Bobby Springer and his family. Amen.* Sport licked J. Michael's cheek with his long, pink, wet tongue.

"J. Michael," a voice called from around the corner of the house. Mr. Fielding, his next-door neighbor, came into sight. "Your mother told me you were back here. I don't mean to bother you, but I'd like to talk with you for a minute. We're going on vacation next week, and I was wondering if you'd take care of our pets while we're away. It would help us out, and maybe the money could help you with your school project."

"Sure! I'd like to if you show me how."

"I'll do that," Mr. Fielding said happily. "I wouldn't leave my dogs with just anyone, you know."

"Well, if you're sure I can do it . . . have you asked my mother if it would be all right?"

"Yes. She said it was fine if you wanted to do it. Come on, I'll show you what needs to be done." The Springer situation would have to wait until some other time.

Mr. Fielding led J. Michael through his house and into a tiny, bright blue laundry room. "You know old Sergeant," Mr. Fielding said, pointing out the window to the dog snoozing under the shade of a large, spreading oak tree. "We have a new puppy too. Mrs. Fielding took him to the vet today for his six-week shots, but I'll introduce you to Snowy before we leave on vacation."

Mr. Fielding unfolded the top of a dog food sack and pulled out a scoop. "Snowy gets one scoop in the red bowl, and Sergeant gets two in the blue bowl."

He led J. Michael out the back screen door and over to the faucet sticking out at the back of the house. Lazy Sergeant barely opened one eye.

"Both dogs drink from this water bucket. Be sure you clean it and fill it with fresh water every day," Mr. Fielding said, as they walked back into the house.

"Is that all I do?" J. Michael asked.

"That's it. You need to feed the dogs once a day, and if you have time, play with them a few minutes. Also, whatever you do, if you go through the back gate into the yard, be sure you close it. Watch Snowy. He'll try to get out."

"No problem. You don't mind if my friend Booker helps me, do you?"

"No, that would be fine. Just take good care of the dogs."

J. Michael thanked Mr. Fielding. He was glad to help the Fieldings, and he really did want his school friends to have computers. He also wanted to help the Springers. His mind drifted off again to little Katie's face and the memory of that old, rusty bus they called home. No shoes. Dirty clothes. No air conditioning. No education. *There has to be some way,* he thought. He thanked the Lord for his clean, comfortable home and Godly family as he crossed the yard and hurried inside.

*   *   *   *   *   *   *

On the first day of the dog-sitting job, both hounds dashed right up to J. Michael when he and Booker opened the back door.

While the dogs hungrily gobbled their dinners, J. Michael went over to fill the water bucket. Snowy ran to stick his nose in the water and almost sneezed as he gulped down the fresh, cool water. He ran around and around, getting tangled in J. Michael's legs before tripping back to his puppy food bowl. The silly little puppy didn't know what to do next. He ran from J. Michael to Booker to his bowl to the bucket and back to J. Michael. Sport—running up and down the fence line—barked playfully from the Kindharts' backyard. He wanted to be a part of the action.

After the dogs' dinner, Booker tried his hand at dog obedience. "Sit, Snowy."

Instead of sitting, Snowy pounced on Booker and licked his nose. *O-o-o-o-oh. Puppy breath.* The sweet smell made Booker want to sneeze. He scratched his nose. "Shake," he commanded again, holding out his hand. The dog ran around him in circles, ears flying.

"He doesn't obey . . . but he likes me, J. Michael!" Booker shouted between giggles. He flopped to the ground, and Snowy crawled over him to get his mouth on Booker's Frisbee™; it looked like something good to chew on. He tried to drag it away from Booker, but Booker pulled back, much to the puppy's surprise. The puppy tugged harder and growled. Booker growled back. The pup stuck his tail straight out and shook his head back and forth to free the captive Frisbee.

"J. Michael, let's play keep-away from Snowy," Booker said. "Here. You go first." Booker gave a final jerk, and the pup had to release it or lose a tooth. Snowy hunched down. He was ready. His eyes fastened on the Frisbee.

J. Michael threw the disk, and it sailed from one side of the yard to the other. "It really floats on the wind today," he said.

Snowy waited for just the right moment. Seeing his opportunity, the dog dashed across the yard, his legs stretched out in hot pursuit of the Frisbee. Booker, too, raced to the spot and dove to the ground, sliding to the Frisbee just in front of the puppy. Good thing he took that baseball stuff seriously. Learning to slide had more than one use!

"Nice try." Booker patted Snowy on the head. Snowy wasn't so sure. Once again Booker sent the disk spinning into the wind. "J. Michael, I can't believe you're getting paid for this. What a great idea! You can have fun and still make money for our project." Just then, the breeze changed directions and carried the whirling Frisbee across the fence into the Fieldings' front yard.

"I'll get it," Booker shouted as he pushed through the gate and ran into the front yard.

"Be careful!" shouted J. Michael. "Don't let Snowy . . . ." But the little, white puppy was too fast. Like a shooting star, he squeezed through the open gateway and was out of sight.

"Snowy . . . Sn-o-o-wy!" J. Michael and Booker called as they chased the puppy down the street. The race was on. The two boys were running with all their might. Their legs began to tingle and feel as weak as jelly. The puppy knew he could win at this game. He was born to run.

"Snowy, come," J. Michael begged as they trailed farther and farther behind.

Finally, Snowy stopped running and trotted teasingly back toward them; then he darted away again. Snowy liked to play by his own rules. He stopped just out of their reach. His busy little tail wagged like a wind-up toy. His merry, dark eyes twinkled as he eyed the two boys and cocked his head to one side.

"He thinks we're playing with him," J. Michael said. "I'll stay here and you try to get behind him," he whispered.

J. Michael knelt down and whistled. Snowy came closer as Booker slowly, soundlessly sneaked around to the side. Suddenly Booker stepped on a twig, and it broke with a loud "snap." The puppy dashed away from both boys. Defeated, J. Michael fell on his back in the grass. Booker gave up too—they were no match for this puppy. After all, he had four legs and they each had only two.

"This isn't working," J. Michael said. "We'll never catch him. What are we going to do? I promised Mr. Fielding that I would take care of his dogs."

"It's not your fault. I'm the one who wasn't careful," Booker said sadly.

J. Michael propped his chin on his knees. Booker pulled a piece of grass off of his shirt and threw it back on the ground.

As the boys thought about what to do next, a man happened to come walking by with a huge, chocolate brown Labrador retriever. He saw the boys sitting in the grass. "Good evening," he greeted, tipping his hat. "Has your pup taken you for a run?"

"No, sir. He ran out of the yard when I opened the gate," Booker explained. "Now we can't catch him. He just wants to play."

"Ah! Maybe that's just the thing to help you catch him," the man said wisely with a sparkle in his eye. He walked over and leaned toward Booker, whispering a plan in his ear. Booker grinned and whispered it to J. Michael.

The two boys jumped up.

"Well, good-bye," the man said. He turned around just in time to avoid hitting a telephone pole that had seemingly jumped into the sidewalk. *Where in the world did I put my glasses? I have to find them.*

J. Michael overdid a loud yawn as he stretched. "Boy, am I tired. Aren't you, Booker?"

"I sure am. Let's go back to your house," Booker said slowly, looking at the puppy out of the corner of his eye.

Booker put his arm across J. Michael's shoulders, and they started talking about other things. Snowy didn't know what to

think. They got nearer the Kindharts' house. Yipping to get the boys' attention, Snowy came closer and closer. It was hard not to look, but if the plan were to work, they had to ignore the puppy. They walked farther and farther down the block, and the puppy came closer and closer. Soon Snowy was leaping and prancing at their feet.

Suddenly, in the middle of a sentence, J. Michael swooped down and snatched up the fluffy ball of fur. Snowy yelped happily and licked the boy's face.

"It worked! It worked!" Booker jumped up and down. "You'll still get the money for the computer."

J. Michael smiled. "And Mr. and Mrs. Fielding still get to keep their dog. That man was smart. He even knows how dogs think. Have you ever seen him before?"

"I don't think so. Maybe he's visiting some friends."

"Yeah. You're probably right . . . probably just visiting some friends." The boys returned the puppy to the backyard and found their Frisbee, which was now autographed by Snowy's deep teeth marks.

"I really am sorry I was careless, J. Michael. Will you forgive me?"

"Sure," J. Michael said as he handed the Frisbee to Booker. "It's your turn to throw now."

CHAPTER 8

STOLEN? . . . FOLLOWED?!

Not everyone had been able to get a fun job like dog-sitting, but they made fun out of their jobs anyway. Many students took jobs collecting cans, throwing newspapers, or even painting fences. Racer persuaded an elderly woman in his mobile home park to allow him to pull weeds in her yard, but he accidentally pulled up a row of her prize tulip bulbs instead. However, she quickly forgave him when he replanted them, and she still paid him for the fine work he did in spotting and pulling other weeds.

It was already the first Saturday morning in July. The sun came up boiling hot. Up and down Ace's street, people busied themselves trying to finish their yard work before it got even hotter. The heat didn't discourage Ace and Racer, though. They opened the lemonade stand extra early, and word spread fast that this was the place to buy a cold drink—and for a good cause too. People kept coming. The most important thing was keeping the pitchers full and the customers happy.

"I'll go in and make more lemonade," Racer said.

"Out of juice already?" Mrs. Virtueson asked with raised brows.

"Yes, ma'am. If we keep it up, Hapford's parents will have to plant another lemon tree!" He quickly set the empty pitcher on the counter and poured in the squeezed juice. As he counted the cups of water, he began to think. *Hm-m . . . We've been open four weeks. July is the middle month of summer. Only a few more weeks to operate a lemonade stand.* Although they had made some profit the last three weeks, the computer fund wasn't growing fast enough, at least not for him. *We could make more profit if we had a way to "stretch" the lemonade. How about less sugar and a little extra water—not much more—just a few more cups?* So he added only half as much sugar and dumped in two extra cups of water before stirring. *What a clever idea. Won't Ace be surprised when the juice lasts*

longer and we make almost twice as much money? He pressed the lid back on the pitcher, grabbed the handle, and carried it back outside.

When Ace took his turn to make up fresh limeade, he followed the recipe exactly and hurried back outside just as one of the neighbors plunked his money down on the stand. "I'll take a cup of that lemonade, please."

The man picked up the cup as soon as Racer filled it, turned it up, and downed it in one big gulp. "U-u-u-g-h!" He bent over coughing. "What is this?" he gasped. The boys shook their heads in surprise. "Well, something's wrong. This stuff tastes terrible—you must have picked some rotten lemons. It's really sour." Racer's eyes darted back and forth from the customer to Ace. *Was it my "special" juice? Surely not . . . maybe the man had just brushed his teeth or something.*

While questions bounced around in Racer's brain, Ace said, "I'm sorry, sir. Here. We'll be happy to exchange it." He gave him a cup of limeade instead. He didn't want to disappoint a good customer. Satisfaction was important, or the customers wouldn't come back.

Most people left right after paying for their lemonade and began drinking it as they walked back to their yards; but when some saw the first man get a new cup, they came back and asked to exchange their cups too. Before long, customers were asking only for limeade. The lemonade just sat untouched.

"Racer," Ace asked when no customers were at the stand, "what happened to this lemonade? Have you tasted it?" Racer looked down at the ground. Ace poured a cup. As soon as he took a sip, he made a face, spit it out, and clutched his throat, choking. "It really does taste awful. What's wrong with it? It's so sour I almost strangled."

"It could be because I put two extra cups of water and not very much sugar in the juice. I wanted to make it go farther," Racer admitted slowly.

"It **could** be?" Ace asked.

"I thought we might make more money for the computer that way." Then pausing, he looked down and mumbled, "I wasted a whole pitcher of juice, didn't I?"

"Racer, I know you were trying to help, but . . ."

"Yes, but I wasn't being honest with the customers."

At that moment, the boys heard footsteps pounding toward them. They turned to see Ronny chasing Susie. He wouldn't stop teasing her, nor would he stop chasing her. She was running very fast, and her face was as red as glowing lava from a volcano. She looked as though she might be ready to explode too! When she angrily turned to look back at him, her foot caught in a crack in the sidewalk, and she fell right into the lemonade stand. Down it went. Down went Susie. Down went the pitchers. Down went the drinks. *Our lemonade stand!* Racer thought. *Just when we were going to get ahead!*

"Now look what you've done, Susie. Leave it to a girl to go and ruin everything," Ronny muttered. Inside, he felt

secretly glad she had knocked over the boys' stand. *Nobody deserves a computer more than me,* he thought.

"Are you all right, Susie?" Ace asked.

"No, she's not all right," Racer said, pointing to her knees. Both were scraped and beginning to bleed. He was now much more concerned for Susie than for the lemonade stand.

"You stay here; I'll get my mother," Ace suggested, starting toward the house.

"Oh, great," Ronny said. "Now I'll get into trouble. Stop crying like a sissy. You didn't fall that hard."

"Go away!" Susie cried. "J-j-just . . . go-o-o . . . away." Surprisingly, he did. Not so surprisingly, it was only because he didn't want to face Mrs. Virtueson when she found out he had caused Susie's fall.

Mrs. Virtueson came outside. "We'd better go wash off those knees and put a little first-aid spray on your scrapes."

"Ow-w-w!" Susie wailed as Mrs. Virtueson helped her walk slowly to the house. Ace and Racer trailed in behind. While all this was happening, no one was watching the lemonade stand. No one except the mysterious man who had slowly turned his dark blue car around the corner. He coasted to a stop at the end of the block and turned off the motor.

Suddenly the man saw a boy taking money out of the money box! The man lifted the camera to get a good picture, checked the lighting, focused, and clicked the red button. It jammed! He tried to click it again. He examined the camera. "Come on," he said under his breath, trying to force the button down. *Dear me! Out of film. Ha! Imagine.* He threw up his hands and then glanced back up at the house. The thief was gone. Not seeing any movement inside, he scribbled a quick note, stepped out onto the sidewalk, dropped the paper into the boys' money box, and then zoomed off down the street.

When Racer and Ace returned to clean up what was left of their stand, Bobby Springer stood there. He gazed at the remains. "Uh . . . Hi," he said, looking at them with

a shy smile. "I was passing by and thought I'd say 'hello.' Looks like a storm blew through." He laughed nervously while shoving his hands in his pockets.

"Two, as a matter of fact," Racer kidded. "One named Ronny and another named Susie."

"You walked all the way here from the bus . . . um-m, I mean, your 'house'?" Ace asked, changing the subject. He and Racer remembered the Springers from the yard sale. In fact, the subject of the Springer family had come up in more than one conversation at the Virtuesons' home. The Virtuesons wanted to make sure the Springers were better off spiritually than they were financially. Pastor Alltruth planned to stop by and see them.

"Naw. I didn't walk all the way here. My pop had to get some bus parts just a few blocks from here. I just walked from the store." He looked around and bit his lip. He tried to think of something else to say.

"There's still a little limeade that didn't run out of the pitcher. Would you like some?" Racer asked. He wanted to do something nice for his new friend. Bobby felt around in his pockets.

"Yeah, well, uh . . . no," Bobby sighed, licking his lips. He longed for just a taste.

"Here, have a cup of limeade for the road—free of charge. I think sales are pretty much over for today anyway," Racer said as he looked over the damage. He figured Bobby really **was** thirsty but didn't have any money.

Bobby drank it all in one gulp. His jaws tightened. It made his hair stand up, but he liked the tingly feeling in his throat. "Well, I'd better head back to the store before my pop leaves me behind! See ya 'round! And thanks for the drink." He left in a flash.

Ace opened the money box and gasped. "We had a whole stack of bills in this box—but look!"

Racer squinted over Ace's shoulder and stared into the box that now contained only small coins. "What happened? Where are they? What's this?" He snatched up a note and read it. His eyes nearly popped out of his head. "Read this," he ordered.

Ace read it quickly. He felt hot all over. His heart pounded; his legs felt as though bubbly soda pop had replaced his blood. He shouted, "Mom!" The boys flew back into the house.

Soon two police cars wheeled into the driveway. One officer jumped out of each car. Neighbors pulled back curtains and peered through peepholes to see what was going on. The Virtuesons' phone nearly rang off the hook, but they were told not to answer it. Though the policemen rarely had time for cases such as this, they made an exception for the Virtuesons. Their good name had earned them a reputation for helping those in need. Now they had a need, and the authorities did not disappoint them.

"Don't worry, Mrs. Virtueson," one of the officers said while he filled out a report.

"I really am sorry to bother you, officer, but the children's money was stolen from their lemonade stand, and a mysterious note was left in the money box. The children seem to think they are being followed."

"Where's the note, son?" an older officer interrupted. Ace handed it to him. "Hm-m," the officer frowned as he read it and scratched his head. The note read,

I've been watching you closely, and I know who took your money. I cannot tell just now, but you'll get it back somehow.

"We're concerned about catching this thief, of course, but the money's not the most important thing here. Someone is following you. See? It says so right here in this note. Do you know who? Or why?" The boys shook their heads.

"Ace, who came to the lemonade stand today? Have you noticed **anyone** unusual . . . anything out of the ordinary?" Mrs. Virtueson asked.

"Well, Ronny spoiled the lemonade stand, but that isn't so unusual or out of the ordinary."

"Maybe Ronny took the money," said Racer.

"But, Racer, Ronny left right after Susie fell down. He didn't want to have to do any explaining." Ace scratched his head and thought some more. "I don't know . . . there was that boy from the edge of town . . . Bobby Springer . . . but he wouldn't have taken that money . . . I don't think. He is very poor, though, . . . and he **was** alone at the stand when we came out of the house."

"Now that I think about it," noted Racer, "he did look uncomfortable."

"That's because he's new around here and he doesn't know us very well. I think he was just shy," said Ace, thinking twice, this time in Bobby's defense.

"You still don't understand, boys. Just as important as who stole the money is who left the note." The officer questioned again, "Who is watching you?"

After a long pause, the officer suggested, "Well, talk to your friends. Your mother tells me you've been spending a lot of time with them lately on this project. Maybe they'll remember something fishy. Regardless," said the officer, "watch your step, boys. We'll be on the lookout for anything unusual."

"Thank you, Officer. I appreciate your coming. We'll let you know if we learn anything new," Mrs. Virtueson promised. She walked the officers to the door. "Racer, get your things; I'll take you home. I don't want you walking home by yourself. I don't think it's safe anymore."

Soon phones began to buzz and ring in Highland City and neighboring Harmony. Mr. Virtueson decided to invite all the children from both schools to meet on Tuesday evening in the fellowship hall at Highland School. Until then, the children searched their brains trying to think who might be watching Ace and Racer—and why.

CHAPTER 9

ANOTHER JIGSAW PUZZLE PIECE

By Tuesday evening everyone had had time to think—maybe too much time. Nearly all had a story to tell and something interesting to share.

"As I recall," mentioned Reginald, "a particular gentleman at the yard sale did ask a question or two about our profits. In my opinion, criminals do like to investigate profits—because it may be a waste of time if the amount of work outweighs the benefits." The other children stared at him. That wasn't anything new. Reginald often spoke in highly sophisticated ways.

Thankfully, Dr. Kindhart spoke up. "But Reginald, anyone could have asked about the profits simply out of kindness. He may have wanted to know how much more money we would need to reach our goal."

"Yes, but this customer had conspicuously big pockets in his pants—good for holding wallets, jewelry, and a money box, I would imagine," Reginald added.

"What did he look like? Did he have a bright red scarf in his jacket pocket, and did he kind of hang around all day?" Pudge broke in. Before Reginald could answer, Miriam chimed in.

"Pudge, you saw him too?" Miriam asked in surprise. "Now that I think of it, he did have a kind of greedy look in his eyes. At first, I thought I was just imagining it."

"What do you mean by that, Miriam?" asked Mrs. Peace.

"Um . . . well, he kept looking around a lot, . . . and he wore big, thick glasses on the end of his nose—like he could be trying to inspect something . . . or steal something . . . like a rat sniffing out a big hunk of cheese. A-a-and he was writing down things on a clipboard—maybe planning a big robbery!" Several girls shivered at the thought.

"Calm down, girls," said Mr. Lovejoy. "Let's think. Unless he was comparing prices with the other yard sales in town, I can't imagine any reason for him to be taking notes half the day."

"He's the criminal," Miriam blurted out again. "I'm sure of it. He looked as if he could be one too. He just paced back and forth and tried not to look anybody in the eye. Criminals hardly ever do, you know. They don't want you to recognize them or to remember their faces. He probably wore that red bandanna-looking thing to wipe off any fingerprints he made on the money box," she added.

"Oh, my!" Sandy put her hands to her head. "Miriam, you just reminded me of something. The man who gave us the extra money at the lemonade stand wiped his face with a red bandanna. Before, I didn't remember exactly what color it was, but now I know. It wasn't pink or orange. It was red! What if the money he gave us was really stolen money? I guess he wanted to encourage us to make money so he would have more money to steal for himself!"

"This is scary!" Christi whispered. "What if he's been watching us the whole summer?"

"You say you remember that he was wearing a red bandanna?" interrupted Booker. Pudge nodded. "J. Michael, remember the man who helped us catch Snowy? His dog had a red rag or handkerchief tied around his neck. Do you suppose . . . ?"

"No," J. Michael stated firmly. "It couldn't have been the same person. Booker, it was only a dog. Lots of dogs wear bandannas. Secondly, the man who helped us was too nice to be a criminal. Besides, he wasn't wearing glasses. He for sure wore no glasses," he said again. "He could have used a good pair, though, now that you mention it. He did almost run into a telephone pole."

"What if he's the same person who left the note in our money box?" Ace asked. "No. No," he answered himself. "Why would he do that if he were trying to steal our money? The note simply said he knew who stole the money . . . not that he took the money."

"Ace, what a perfect trick!" Racer exclaimed, throwing up his hands. "Don't you get it? He's trying to mislead us or give us the wrong idea. He wouldn't tell us if he were the criminal. Right?"

"Wait one moment." Reginald's mind raced. "Let's solve this puzzle by putting all the pieces together logically. What was it you said the other day about Bobby Springer?"

"What about him?" Racer asked.

"He was the only individual standing at the lemonade stand when you came back outside. Is that correct?" Ace and Racer nodded their heads. "So you had the money before he came, and after he left, it was gone," Reginald continued. "Well, it seems like simple, logical, deductive reasoning to me. Bobby Springer is the one who took the money! Mystery solved." Reginald sat back and crossed his arms in satisfaction.

"I don't believe it," J. Michael said boldly. At least he didn't want to believe it. "Now that we're on the subject of the Springers, I wish we could give them some money to buy food or clothes, or to fix their 'house,' or to go to school. I know God didn't bring them into our lives unless it was for a reason. God might be using the Springers and this theft to make us take our minds off what we want for ourselves and focus on their needs instead."

A long pause followed.

"Could be," Ace thoughtfully nodded.

"Maybe we need a benevolence fund," suggested Reginald.

"A benevo-wh-a–t?" asked Hapford, knitting his eyebrows. Hapford did not share Reginald's love for big words.

"You know," replied Reginald. "A benevolence fund . . . when you set money aside to help someone—in this case, the Springers. Sadly, at present, no extra funds exist in the account." He quickly did some math in his head; then he shook it as though the decision were final.

"We still have **some** computer money that wasn't stolen . . ." Ace trailed off. He knew not everyone would like what he was thinking. What he said was loud enough for Pudge to hear, though.

"Oh, no, you don't! That money is for our school computers. We're not going to give it away. Maybe the Springers do need the money, but so do we. That's why we all agreed to work this summer."

"Yes, Pudge, but their need is greater than ours," Sandy said.

"Don't even think about it, Ace," Pudge warned.

Booker broke in. "I'm with you, Pudge. We've worked too hard to stop now."

"What if we gave the Springers the money we make at the Founders' Day bake sale? Would that be fair?" Christi asked.

"But that may be our biggest fund raiser of the whole summer," grumbled Pudge. "If we don't keep that money, we won't have enough to buy the computers, and we will have worked the whole summer for nothing."

"Wait a minute, Pudge," Ace said. "We can share."

"Yes, Pudge," Christi added. "Any time we give something in His name, it's as if we are giving it to the Lord. That's not for nothing." Pudge's conscience got the better of him. He got the message.

The parents remained silent. The students would solve this problem on their own. They understood God's Spirit speaking in their lives, but following Him wasn't always easy.

Ace looked from one friend to another. "If you would be willing to donate the bake sale money to the Springers, raise your hand." J. Michael's went up first, then Christi's, Sandy's, and Reginald's. Racer, Miriam, and Hapford checked around before joining in. Reluctantly, Pudge and Booker raised their hands too. They knew it was the right thing to do. It was settled.

The only things not settled now were who stole the money from the lemonade stand and who could be following them. The students had no real proof or explanation to point a finger at anyone. Just looking around at a garage sale, walking a dog, or giving a little money to a lemonade stand was no crime. No one had actually seen the person who stole the money. They needed more proof and more agreement on the mystery man's description. Everybody remembered seeing a red scarf, or handkerchief, or rag, or bandanna; but no one could really describe the man. It seemed everyone remembered something different. Instead of completing the puzzle, it only added more questions.

At least the students did agree to sacrifice part of their hard-earned money to give to the Springers. That was the most important thing right now. Because it was God's leading, He would bless them for it. All the other things would take care of themselves— in God's time and in God's way. So that was the end of that . . . for now.

CHAPTER 10

WAGS DOES HIS PART

Measure . . . pour . . . mix . . . bake. Measure . . . pour . . . mix . . . bake. After several days of hearing nothing more about the mysterious note or the criminal, things seemed somewhat back to normal. The students returned to the project of raising money for computers and the Springers.

Mrs. Virtueson invited Christi, Miriam, Sandy, Racer, and Pudge to make their baking headquarters in her kitchen. Pudge helped sprinkle flour on the cookie dough, as well as on the floor, while Racer cut the dough into interesting shapes and sizes.

"Hm-m . . . I think I need to sample this. It may not be good enough to sell," Pudge said, sticking a glob of cookie dough in his mouth.

"Pudge!" Sandy warned. "Stop that!"

"Huh?" Pudge looked up. Christi giggled.

"Are your cookies ready to go into the oven, Racer?" Mrs. Virtueson looked on and

smiled. Racer nodded and handed over the cookie sheet. Mrs. Virtueson popped them in, and Christi peeked through the oven window every now and then to make sure they weren't getting too brown.

"I like lots of icing on my cookies," Miriam said as she squirted some fresh-baked cookies (and her dress) with the messy decorating tube. "I can make pictures and faces on these cookies," she said.

Next came the gooey chocolate chip cookies, peanut butter drops, and homemade brownies. Ace took a turn using the mixer until all the lumps were gone. "Whoa!" he yelled as Pudge pulled the metal blades up before the mixer had completely stopped.

"Oh, Pudge. Look at the wall . . . and the cookbooks . . . and the counter . . . and the floor." Christi's voice got lower and lower as she put her hand to her mouth. Pudge sheepishly glanced around to see chocolate splotches decorating the kitchen.

"Don't worry. I'll lick them up," Pudge told Mrs. Virtueson.

"Oh, no, you won't," she declared before playfully tossing him a checkered dishcloth. "Here, use this after you wet it in the sink." He repentantly accepted it and began cleaning up.

Racer scraped the last of the cookies off the metal sheets. He could not seem to stop crumbs from flying to the floor.

Next came the pies. Racer said he'd like to make pie crusts. "What are you supposed to put into a pie anyway?" he asked.

"Your teeth," Pudge grinned. Racer licked his lips. He had never made one before, but how hard could it be?

"What kind of pie are you going to make, Racer?" Sandy asked.

"Oh, I don't know. My mother told me never to tell until after it was already cooked. That way, her apple pie can become an apple upside-down treat or a browned apple crisp, and no one will ever know the difference!"

Mrs. Virtueson laughed. "So that's why your mom's such a good cook. I'll have to remember that, Racer. Thanks for the tip."

Racer patted the dough down with his hands and used the rolling pin to make it flat. The dough was much stickier than he'd thought. Not seeing another rag, he wiped the extra dough on his apron. *Better than wiping it on my pants,* he reasoned. He pulled the dough off the rolling pin, dusted it with more flour, and scooped out a little extra to put on top of the dough. When he rolled it out again, he was proud of himself because the dough didn't seem quite so sticky this time—at least not on top anyway. He picked up the dough to place it in the pan, but somehow the center of the dough didn't follow the edges into the pan. It stayed glued to the counter. He was holding a large doughnut ring that stretched further each second. "Aw-w-w," he moaned.

By the time the first pie crust was placed in the glass dish and pinched around the edges, Racer looked like an angel wearing an apron! He was covered from head to toe in white flour!

It had been a busy day; a mountain of cookies and brownies proved it. While the girls finished boxing up the goodies, Mrs. Virtueson made phone calls to let parents know the children were ready to go home. Ace zipped outside to get a bucket to clean the floor. While Ace was outside, however, Racer thought of a faster way to clean the floor and surprise Ace's mom. "Sh-h-h!" he motioned to the others. Tiptoeing over to the door and cracking it open, he knelt down and called, "Here, Wags. Here, boy!"

"Um-m," Miriam paused. "I don't think that's such a good idea, Racer." Racer didn't listen. Good ol' Wags bounded into the kitchen, hungry for an afternoon snack. Never did he imagine such a treat! He skidded and slid from spot to spot . . . his tail making half circles in the flour. He liked the chocolate chip cookie crumbs and leftover sugar cookie dough the best. Suddenly Mrs. Virtueson and Ace walked back in. Uh-oh. The smudge of red icing on the end of Wag's nose gave him away. Even Mrs. Virtueson couldn't help laughing.

"Wags, you look like a sundae with a cherry on top!" She grabbed hold of his collar and pulled the unwilling pup to the door. "Come on, Wags. Get out of here before I have to put you on a diet!" She turned back toward the wide-eyed children staring at her. "Now the rest of you can work up some elbow grease cleaning this floor. The cleaner is under the sink, Racer. I'll bring you a mop, Pudge. You'll have plenty of time before your parents get here." She smiled. They all understood.

"Way to go, Racer," Pudge remarked. "Baking was work, but mopping up is even more work."

"We can take turns," Christi said.

"We needed to scrub the floor anyway, after the mess we made," added Miriam.

Mrs. McMercy had agreed to deliver all the cookies to the booth the next day for the sale, so she took the cookies home with her. When Sandy's brother Bill came home, the unmistakable smell of cinnamon and brown sugar met him at the door and led him into the kitchen. The cookies seemed to be calling to him. He decided to eat just one. "M-m-m-m. Heavenly." Then he decided to eat just one more. Next thing he knew, one whole package was gone!

With his mouth full of cookies, Bill looked like a chipmunk. Sandy walked by and saw the crumbs at the corners of his mouth.

"Bill, what are you eating? The cookies for our bake sale?" Sandy cried. Guilt was written all over his face.

Bake sale? Now Bill remembered. "Sandy, I'm really sorry. I know I should have asked before I sampled them, but they looked so-o good. Will you forgive me? Please, please? I'll tell you what, Sandy. Those cookies were so good I'll pay for the ones I ate. In fact, I'll pay you double. Then you'll make twice the money you'd get if I hadn't eaten any of them. How would that be?"

Sandy kept looking at the floor. She really loved her big brother, and she knew forgiving him was the right thing to do. Slowly she said, "I forgive you, Bill. The money was for the computer project, but we've decided to donate it to the Springers. Now you have played a part in helping us raise the money too."

CHAPTER 11

THE PARADE AND THE WIRE

Celebrating the founding of Highland City, people swarmed everywhere—in the streets and all around the craft tables, snack booths, and art exhibits. Children weaved in and out of a maze of legs, and customers gathered around the brightly decorated bake sale booth.

"How much are these brownies?" a voice rang out.

People were standing three and four deep on all three sides of the booth. "Hurry up; I'm thirsty," a little boy begged.

"Let's make a couple of lines, please," Mrs. Peace suggested, raising her voice. "If you only want something to drink, line up over there. If you want food or food and drinks, line up here. We'll take care of you as quickly as we can." There were so many customers the wrapped goodies were almost sold out.

Far down the street, a brass band began to play. The sounds of whistling flutes,

tooting horns, and crashing cymbals filled the air. Puffy-haired clowns dressed in polka-dotted suits and oversized shoes cleared the street for the coming band. One happy clown let a little fellow smell a blue plastic flower ring he held, but when the little boy sniffed, the flower squirted water in his face! The boy squealed and clapped his hands. He wanted to do it again, but the clown was already moving on to spot his next target!

Miriam and Sandy stood on the sturdy ice chest so they could see. Mrs. McMercy steadied Becky on a wobbly chair. Band members dressed in navy blue and white uniforms came first, stepping high as they marched in long, straight lines. Behind them, the mayor of Highland City waved and zigzagged back and forth in a shiny red sports car.

Next came the teddy bear parade! Children tugged wagonloads of stuffed animals past the sea of faces. Streamers twisted and twirled in the breeze. A barrel train chugged from behind in figure eights. Purple. Green.

Red. Yellow. Blue. Each barrel was a different color and seated two children . . . and sometimes a doll. The conductor blew his old brass whistle as he came to the end of each block.

"Oh, look!" Becky cried. "I want to ride. May I, Mommy, may I?"

All eyes were fixed on the parade because next came the floats. People all over were taking pictures—of this band, of that car, of those children. One man, dressed as a clown, pulled a camera out of a bright red scarf and began taking pictures of the bake sale booth. When a small boy tugged his sleeve to shake his hand, the clown decided he'd taken enough pictures and slipped the camera back into his suit.

The first float had a banner that read, "Changing the World One Child at a Time." A huge globe—painted blue, green, and brown like Earth—rested in the center of the float. The words School of Tomorrow® sparkled in shimmering gold letters around the bottom edges of the float. Hapford sat in an office and pretended to work in a

PACE; Booker sat at a computer and pretended to type. Circling the globe, uniformed students from Harmony and Highland Schools stood shoulder to shoulder. They waved to the crowd. To the rear of the float, the color guard marched in their perfectly pressed uniforms and white gloves. Cheers, shouts, and whistles sprang out from the lively crowd. Two students jumped off the float to help at the bake sale booth.

Next came the riding club. A chestnut mare shook her head as she pranced. One rosy-cheeked cowboy on a red-and-green saddle blanket circled a lasso high above his head. A woman in high, lace-up boots and a long, silky dress rode on an old-fashioned sidesaddle. Her horse's mane and tail were braided with bright blue and gold ribbons.

At the end of the parade, an old farm truck overflowing with hay rambled along. Well, not just hay. Tiny heads—with hair full of grass and bits of straw—bobbed up and down. The children hiding in the hay popped up and down as they threw handfuls of candy to scrambling children waiting eagerly on the sides of the street.

As quickly as the parade had come, it was over.

Without warning, a harsh, high-pitched voice tore through the contented chatter that followed the parade. "Hey, you cheated me! You didn't give me enough change!"

Mrs. Peace turned toward a surprised and confused Miriam.

"What seems to be the problem?" Mrs. Peace asked as she stepped up behind Miriam.

"She didn't give me enough change," the angry woman scolded, pointing at Miriam. Her loud voice was attracting much attention.

"I did give her the right change, Mother. I was really careful. Honest, I was." Miriam's nose tingled and her vision blurred as tears formed in the corners of her eyes. She didn't want anyone to think she was too young or too careless to be handling money.

"How much change did she give you?" Mrs. Peace asked.

"I gave her a ten-dollar bill to break down into ones before the parade started, but she only gave me change for a five. I just noticed. Money doesn't grow on trees, you know."

Mrs. Peace reached for the money box. It was gone! "Miriam, did you move the money box?" Mrs. Peace questioned. "I don't see it."

"No, I didn't do anything with it," Miriam replied honestly. "Maybe Mrs. McMercy knows where it is."

"Mrs. McMercy," Mrs. Peace called out, "do you know where the money box is? I can't seem to find it."

"Right under the counter," Mrs. McMercy said. But the money box wasn't right under the counter.

"I've already looked," said Mrs. Peace with an edge of concern in her voice. She looked the customer in the eye. "I'm sure it was just a simple mistake. Here." She reached for her purse and gave the customer five dollars from her own wallet.

"Hm-pf-f!" the woman muttered as she pranced away in triumph. Mrs. Peace sat down with Miriam, while the other girls closed up the stand.

"I was very careful," Miriam said.

"Honey, I believe you. I gave her the money to please God." She thought for a moment. "It's a good thing we're about to close. We can't give anyone change until we find that money box. Did you see anyone move it?"

"No, ma'am. I was watching the parade. I thought you were watching the money box." Miriam's shoulders slumped further—the disappearance of the money box discouraged her even more as she thought about the hurtful words of that woman. Mrs. Peace could tell.

"I don't mean to interrupt," said Mrs. McMercy, walking up, "but we're almost ready to leave. Everything has been packed back into boxes, but we haven't found the money box yet."

Miriam leaned over and buried her head in her mother's arms. Mrs. Peace stroked Miriam's hair. "Let's just pray someone finds it and returns it. Somehow God will supply," Mrs. Peace said.

"We will pray," said Mrs. McMercy. "We won't worry about it. God will see that we get that money back if He wants us to have it. Thank you for your hard work, Miriam, and thank you, Mrs. Peace, for all your help."

After Miriam and Mrs. Peace wished the McMercys farewell and had a word of prayer together, they thought over the events of the day . . . the parade . . . the floats . . . the booth . . . . *The money we earned to give to the Springers is gone!* Miriam closed her eyes and shook her head. *Who would do such a thing?*

Crash! Clatter! Clatter! Startled, Miriam and Mrs. Peace looked up. Something dropped to the ground across the street. Mrs. Peace noticed something slipping across the pavement. "It's not an extension cord. Why, it's a wire! It looks like a microphone wire!" she exclaimed under her breath. Looking toward the thin wire, they could see only a pair of legs behind a parked car.

Someone was trying to pull back the wire. Whoever it was had squatted down low, as he tried somewhat unsuccessfully not to be seen. He gave the wire a few more jerks and managed to yank it out of sight. Dismayed by his own carelessness, the man stood and rushed away through the crowd.

"There he is! That's him!" Miriam cried. "The man with the red rag! He has clown make-up smeared on his face!" She wanted to go after him, but her mother held her back. The man hurriedly covered a small tape recorder to hide it from view. He stuffed it into a white paper sack out of which hung part of a clown suit. "I think he's the one who took our money box!" she cried.

"It's okay, Miriam," said Mrs. Peace. "Settle down."

No, it's not okay, Miriam thought, trying desperately to remain self-controlled.

Once the man disappeared, Mrs. Peace got up from her chair and walked cautiously toward the parked car a few yards away.

She stooped down and picked up something square and black.

"Aha!" Mrs. Peace remarked. "We have him now. Finally, a piece of evidence!"

"What is it, Mother?" asked Miriam.

"A mini-cassette!"

"I didn't even see it!" Miriam gasped. "Let's play it, Mom!"

"Not now, dear. We're going to take it home to your father."

CHAPTER 12

REWIND!

The Highland School fellowship hall was packed. It was time to play the secret tape. By this time, everyone knew the story of how Mrs. Peace and Miriam had found it, and they watched closely as Mr. Peace put it into the recorder.

Having listened to the tape, the parents now needed the children's input to help it all make sense. "No doubt the criminal will be missing this tape soon; and when he comes back to look for it, we'll be ready. Go ahead and play it for them, Mr. Virtueson," said Mr. Peace, a lawyer. Mr. Virtueson hit the PLAY button. All they could hear were hissing sounds. It was hard to make out anything at first. Then, "with even more things to do. . . . God will help us find ways to make money, if we ask for His help and are ready to work hard."

"That's me!" Ace shouted. "That's when we were in the park where I first introduced the idea of the computer project,

129

remember?" Happy and Christi nodded their heads. Racer strained to hear more on the tape. CLICK. More crackling. Suddenly, "I only hope we have enough time to make all the money we need to pay for a whole computer." Booker's eyes grew big as saucers. "How much does one cost, anyway? More than we have in our piggy banks," a voice trailed off on the machine.

"How did he do that?" Booker frowned. "J. Michael, that was at the baseball field. You had just shared the idea with me about raising money. I don't remember seeing anyone strange, do you? Man, this guy is sneaky!"

"Maybe that's why he's a criminal," said Hapford out loud.

More brushing noises. "How about some punch?"

Christi gasped.

"We'll just pour all the juice into one cup, and you can have it at half price."

"How dare he record what I said!" Christi said in horror. "He didn't even ask my permission!"

"No," Ace replied. "Criminals usually don't ask permission. That's why they're criminals." Christi held her tongue.

The tape continued. When the breeze blew, it sounded like tissue paper rubbing over the head of the microphone. Individual words blurred together. Voices came close and faded away. Silence. More silence. "A-a-u-g-h-h-h!" a girl screamed. "Oh, Mommy, help me! Please, help me!" The children looked at each other and J. Michael yelled out, "Katie!"

"That was at the yard sale. Remember the man taking notes?" said Racer.

"Phew! I've never smelled anything so bad." They all laughed, remembering Sandy and the skunk spray. They heard a series of muffled sounds, like people rushing past the microphone; then the person moved closer to little Katie.

"Take off your tennis shoes, Katie. I don't think we can save them."

"No, . . . it's the only pair I have."

A long pause followed. Then loud steps rushed toward the microphone. A second set of steps dashed past. "Oh!" another girl cried. A man gasped. Many voices started talking at the same time.

"Ow-w-w!" a voice cried.

"Who is that?" Miriam asked.

"Sh-h!" whispered Ace.

"I'd recognize Susie's whine anywhere," Racer said. "Remember when she and Ronny crashed into the lemonade stand?"

"Sh-h-h, someone's talking," Sandy said. They could hear a man whispering, but they couldn't make out his words. Footsteps. Someone whistling. The recorder suddenly cut off on that side.

"We do know one thing," Miriam added. "We've all seen a man with a red rag, cloth, or scarf, right? Well, today, when he dropped the tape, we saw him folding a red piece of material around a microphone as he hurried away. That's how he's been recording us. He's hiding the microphone behind that red material!" The rest of the tape contained bits and pieces of conversation but nothing to reveal the name of the man with the red handkerchief. The tape proved someone was following them, but who? Why? None of the students knew. On top of that, the Springers had been told about the project and the money gift. Now, who would tell them about the stolen money from the bake sale? No one wanted to be the one to break the disappointing news.

CHAPTER 13

THE CURIOUS SNAPSHOT

Ace, Miriam, Christi, and J. Michael rode with Mr. Peace and Mr. Lovejoy to the Springers' bus home at the edge of town.

Katie came running out of the bus first, followed by Bobby and their mother, who seemed to have given more attention to her hair and clothes than when the children had seen her last. She recognized them right away.

"Hello," she greeted them politely.

"Good afternoon, Mrs. Springer," said Ace. "You remember J. Michael, Miriam, and Christi, don't you?"

"Oh, of course," she smiled.

"This is Mr. Peace, Miriam's dad, and Mr. Lovejoy, Christi's father."

"It's nice to meet you," she smiled. Ace paused and tried to collect his thoughts. He was a little down about having to tell the Springers that the money they needed wasn't available.

"I'm afraid we have some sad news," Ace broke the silence. "Would you like to explain, Miriam?"

Miriam swallowed the growing lump in her throat. She smiled weakly and began. "Mrs. Springer, we're here because . . . we're here because . . . well, we were all watching the parade. I was, Sandy was, Sandy's mom, and my mom too. There was so much to see that we weren't paying close attention to the money box. We never dreamed anything would happen . . . with all of us standing in broad daylight. It was the most money we've made all summer," her voice broke.

"Yes?" Mrs. Springer leaned forward trying to understand where Miriam was going with this speech.

"You see," J. Michael continued, "sometime between the time the parade started and when it ended, somebody stole the money box out of our booth."

"Oh . . . I see," Mrs. Springer said quietly. She stared at the ground.

Katie tugged gently at her mother's thin skirt. "Does that mean I won't be getting new clothes?" She looked at her mother and then at the children and then at the parents. Christi's stomach twisted in a knot.

Mrs. Springer nodded her head slowly. "Well," she said trying to cover her disappointment, "thank you for trying. I know you wanted to help. You've been good to us. We do appreciate . . ."

"Hey, what are you all doing over here?" Ronny asked curiously as he skidded to a stop on his bike. Loose gravel sprayed the bottom of Ace's feet.

Ace said evenly, "We were just telling the Springers the bad news about the bake sale."

"What bad news?" Ronny asked. He acted as if he knew nothing.

"Somebody stole all the money we made," Ace said, "not only from the bake sale booth but also from the lemonade stand. It's extra bad because we were going to give the money we earned at the bake sale to the Springers."

"A-a-w-w-w. That's too bad," Ronny said. He looked a little too sad to be believable. "I mean, that's too bad about the bake sale, but I know who stole the money from your lemonade stand," he added with a gleam in his eyes.

"You do?" Christi almost yelled, her eyes bugging out. "Tell us. Tell us!"

Ronny pointed a finger at Bobby Springer.

Ace looked at J. Michael. J. Michael looked at Ace. Christi felt sick. Surely it wasn't true. It couldn't be. This is what they had feared. Bobby Springer was the one who had been standing by the lemonade stand when Ace and Racer came back outside from helping Mrs. Virtueson with Susie. He had looked nervous and uncomfortable, but the students couldn't bring themselves to believe that Bobby would do such a thing.

"He did it," Ronny barked.

"I did not," Bobby frowned. His fingers began to curl up into a fist. "I never stole any money in my life. I may not be the smartest kid in town, but I know the difference between right and wrong, and I wouldn't steal." His stomach tightened, and the muscles in his legs tensed.

Mr. Peace stepped between the two boys and questioned, "How do you know Bobby took the money, Ronny?"

"Well, I was chasing Susie down the sidewalk, and she fell and hit the lemonade stand. Racer, Ace, and Mrs. Virtueson went in to fix Susie's scraped knees. And . . . well . . . while they were gone, I saw Bobby take the money."

"I thought you left when Susie told you to go away," Ace jumped into the conversation. Ronny gave him a mean look and turned his head.

"You mean you didn't try to stop him?" asked Mr. Lovejoy.

Ronny sputtered and threw his arms up in the air. "No. I didn't know what to do. I'm only a kid."

Mrs. Springer looked very hurt. "Go back into the house, Bobby Joseph Springer. There will be no more about this until your father gets home."

Bobby turned obediently but pleaded, "Mother, please don't believe him. I never took the money. You know I wouldn't do that." Blood rushed to his head. He didn't know which hurt the most—Ronny's words or his mother's look of disappointment. "I just went by to say 'hi.' That's all. I promise."

Ace wished he could crawl into a hole; he felt so helpless. J. Michael wished he were invisible. Christi wanted to help, but she didn't know how. *I wish I hadn't come here,* Miriam thought.

"Just a minute, Mrs. Springer. Let Bobby stay while we hear this story out," Mr. Peace said. "I'm not yet convinced Bobby did anything wrong. Ronny, just because Bobby was standing by the lemonade stand doesn't prove he took the money."

"But I saw him with twenty-five dollars in his hand!" Ronny almost yelled.

Ace asked quietly, "How did you know twenty-five dollars was in the money box,

Ronny? I never said how much money we lost."

Whoops!

Just then a car horn honked behind the little group. Everyone turned to see a dark blue car that had pulled up quietly. Still tucking in his shirt and smoothing his hair, a stranger jumped out and quickly walked toward the group. His thick glasses could explain why his tie and suspenders didn't match too well, but he looked like a kind person. The man cleared his throat.

"I have some information that may interest all of you. I happened to be at the Founders' Day parade taking a few pictures. When I developed my film, I found a very strange photo among them. You might be interested to see it." Ronny looked away, uninterested. The gentleman handed the mysterious photo to Mr. Peace. Mr. Peace held it close and squinted his eyes.

"I see," said the lawyer slowly. "Thank you, sir." He shook the man's hand. "We'll take it from here." Mr. Peace didn't ask any more questions, and the stranger didn't give any answers.

"As you wish," said the gentleman. He turned to hop back into the car. Ace thought he caught a glimpse of something red on the car seat, but before he could say anything, Mr. Peace began speaking again and the car sped off.

"Ronny, you say you counted out twenty-five dollars by the lemonade stand?"

"Yes," Ronny said slowly. "I mean no. I didn't count out twenty-five dollars. Bobby did."

"Tell me," Mr. Peace said, holding out the picture, "how much money did you count out of this money box?"

Ronny frowned and looked at the picture. "I don't understand what you mean," he stuttered. All of a sudden he had nothing to say.

"Take a good look at the booth in this picture. Do you notice anything unusual?" Mr. Peace moved the photo closer to Ronny so he could have a better look.

Ronny pretended to look at it. "No," he lied.

"Look again," Mr. Lovejoy suggested.

Ronny looked a little closer. "I see some girls watching a parade; that's all," he lied again.

"What about the boy in the picture? The boy with a money box in his hands. Do you recognize him?"

"Uh, maybe. Maybe I've seen him around before. I can't really be sure."

"Ronny, you were at that parade, weren't you?" Mr. Peace questioned. "While the girls were watching the floats go by, you sneaked in the back and took the money box, didn't you?" Ronny said nothing.

"In fact," Mr. Lovejoy added, "the bicycle leaning up against the side of the booth looks strangely like the one you're sitting on right now." Ronny was silent. His ears burned bright red.

Mr. Lovejoy looked at Mr. Peace. Mr. Peace looked at the children. The children looked at Ronny. Ronny looked at the ground. No one knew what to say.

CHAPTER 14

CAUGHT!

Thanks to the man in the blue car who had come up at just the right minute, the thief had been caught. The parents decided they wouldn't call the authorities if Ronny returned all the money—from the bake sale and the lemonade stand. He seemed sorry— sorry he had been caught, that is. With the money back, however, the students happily turned over a big portion to the Springers. When they saw the beaming faces of Katie, Bobby, and Mrs. Springer, no doubt remained that they had done the right thing.

Nevertheless, summer was over. They wouldn't have the new computers they had worked so hard to earn, but none of them complained. They would still work on Saturdays until cold weather came, and they would put aside the money they earned until sometime in the future when they had enough to buy computers.

Saturday afternoon, the children met back at the park, where the project had begun.

Knowing they were going to give short testimonies the next evening at School Night, they were rehearsing what to say. The pastors from both churches had planned a combined School Night to start off the year. Each student planned to share one thing he or she had learned during the summer.

"Pudge, you're rambling," said Racer. "Get to the point." Pudge glanced at Mrs. Virtueson, who made sure he kept within the given time limit.

"I wonder what's up?" J. Michael interrupted. He pointed to a police car rolling to a stop. Mrs. Virtueson noticed, too, but said nothing. Pudge was still practicing.

"Come out with your hands up!" a voice boomed over a loudspeaker. The students looked at Mrs. Virtueson. Mrs. Virtueson looked at the students. They all looked at the policeman. Another squad car screeched to a halt before almost hitting the first one. A second officer stepped out to help his partner. His shiny badge sparkled in the afternoon sun.

"You—behind the tree—move out," said the first officer. Happy rubbed his eyes. Sandy grabbed Christi's hand. Slowly, from behind a thick, old oak tree, a man with a red handkerchief in his pocket appeared. He had what looked like a notebook in his hand. Miriam's hand flew to her mouth. The boys stood frozen. Only a squirrel moved as it raced up the trunk of a tree.

The officer pointed to the man's notebook. "Drop it on the ground," he commanded. The man released it, and it fell to the ground. He quickly turned away from the children and faced the officers.

One officer spoke to the children and Mrs. Virtueson. "It's all right, young people. Just move over next to 'Mom' and nobody will get hurt."

The other officer looked at the man. "Put your hands behind your back and don't try to pull any stupid stunts, mister. The game's up. It's all over. Children, this is the man who has been following you."

"Wait!" Christi cried out. She gave the man a hard look again. Even from the back, she was sure she recognized him. It was the man who had given them the photo of Ronny stealing the money. *He's not the criminal!* she realized. "Let him go! He's the man who caught the thief who stole from us. He gave us the picture. Without his help, the Springers never would have gotten the money!"

"Sorry, sweetie, but this man isn't a hero, at least not in my book. We fingerprinted the photo he gave you and matched it with the fingerprints on the cassette tape. They're the same. He's the one who has been following you. You just never saw him up close." The man hung his head. Christi was confused. The officer hurriedly put the handcuffs on the man and led him to the squad car. The officer picked up the notebook, and the police car raced off to the police station. Christi stared at the red and blue lights flashing as the police car disappeared.

CHAPTER 15

FOUND OUT!

Sitting in church Sunday morning, at least two young people had a hard time concentrating. Christi was thinking more about the man who had been following them than she was about the words of the hymns. Even Ace, who was usually very attentive, caught his mind drifting off the sermon a time or two. *Could that man really have meant us harm? Maybe someone will know something by School Night tonight.* It didn't seem right to go back to school the next day with such a riddle unsolved.

Getting ready for School Night, Pudge struggled with his uniform tie. It didn't look right. He twisted and pulled. The students would all be wearing their uniforms, and Pudge wanted to look his best, but . . . he wasn't sure he was ready to start back to school. It was just . . . it was just that . . . he had wanted to start the school year off right—with brand-new computers.

Sandy and Becky were dressed in their uniforms and were now brushing their hair to get ready. J. Michael fed Sport and gave him an extra scoop of food and one last hug before leaving. Booker put up his baseball cap, Miriam tied the last bow in her hair, Hapford brushed his teeth, and Reginald gathered notebook paper in case he needed to take some useful notes.

Mr. and Mrs. Virtueson were strangely quiet, and the Kindharts didn't have much to say either as all headed for School Night. Even Mrs. Meekway was unusually thoughtful.

By the time students and parents arrived for School Night, however, it seemed they all had put summer behind and were ready to launch into a new school year. Cars pulled up. Doors opened and closed. Pastor Alltruth and Pastor Gentle greeted everyone as the auditorium filled with chatting parents and giggling children. Some children could hardly sit still.

"This is my first year going to a 'real' school," one girl said proudly.

"I can't wait to make new friends!" said another as she swung her legs back and forth under the pew.

"Be still and fold your hands," the child's mother said gently.

Pastor Alltruth stepped to the pulpit. "Boys and girls, I know you're eager to get back to school. Your schoolwork probably won't be as difficult as the hard work some of you've already been doing this summer," he laughed. "We are pleased to welcome you back to school and so glad to have all of your parents here. Do you remember the Springers?"

Ace remembered. He recalled Katie asking Jesus to come into her heart. He smiled as Pastor Alltruth continued.

"At one time the Springers had attended a small church and heard the Gospel. But we know going to church doesn't make you a Believer any more than sitting in a garage makes you a car! This time they not only recognized their need for God, but they, each one, confessed Jesus as Lord and asked Him to be their personal

Saviour. I guess that's when the good word came for Mr. Springer. Permanent work awaits him as soon as he arrives in California. I believe God is pleased. I am also. By the grace of God and the generosity of you students, they repaired that old bus and got it ready for the trip yesterday. You helped them do something they couldn't do themselves.

"Now, for a second item of interest. The police did, in fact, catch the man who has been following some of you." Several students looked back and forth at one another.

"Is he a bad guy?" Becky asked, elbowing Sandy.

"Sh-h," Sandy replied.

"What are they going to do with him?" Pudge whispered to Reginald.

"Maybe they discovered he was a foreign spy. They will, by all probabilities, deport him out of the country," Reginald whispered back.

"They're bringing him here to church this evening," Pastor Gentle announced.

W-H-A-T? Pudge yelled on the inside. Miriam thought she might faint.

A criminal is coming? Hapford wanted to hide behind a chair.

I-I don't think my parents will like that, Sandy thought to herself.

Reginald wondered, *Did the criminal profess to becoming a Believer or something?* Even Reginald seemed somewhat confused, and that **was** unusual.

"Don't worry. Everything is fine. They'll be coming later," Pastor Alltruth added. Sandy frowned and raised one eyebrow.

"Until they get here," the pastor continued, "we want to get to know our new school families, and we'd like to hear some testimonies. Pastor Gentle, come and start things off, please."

"I'd like to ask all the staff and students from Harmony School to come and stand to my right." The young people quickly marched to the front. "Aren't they a fine group of young people?" Pastor Gentle said. "Let's give all the folks from Harmony a big hand." Clapping echoed through the auditorium. "Now all you Highland School students come and stand with your staff over here. We asked all of you to be here tonight to celebrate and to thank the Lord for what He has done this summer. Because of the faith and vision of these young people to work hard, to raise money, and to leave the results to God, we have all learned some important lessons.

"Some of our young people would like to share a few of those lessons. Racer, you lead the way." *Oh, I really didn't want to be first*, Racer thought, but he threw back his shoulders and walked over to the pulpit. Ace bravely followed.

"Um. Good evening. Um . . . I'm Racer Loyalton. This summer I learned that sometimes we have to wait and be patient to see the results of our work. That wasn't an easy lesson for me." He coughed and hurried to sit down.

Then Ace stepped forward. "I learned that it takes much thought and planning to start a business; it doesn't just happen. I began to understand how hard my parents work to allow me to come to this school. Thanks, Dad and Mom." His mother winked at him as she remembered the lemonade stand.

The students began to relax as several others spoke up. "I learned that people are more important than goals, computers, or money," said J. Michael.

Sandy smiled and said, "It was really fun to work together and surprising to see how much every little bit helps when we each do our part."

Pudge blushed and tried to straighten his tie again. "I remember my bad attitude when we started this whole thing. I'm thankful God sent me friends who encouraged me and helped me do something that made me feel good about myself."

Just then the door at the side of the platform opened. In walked two policemen and the "criminal." His hands were behind his back. The boys were sure he was handcuffed.

"Excuse me," Pastor Alltruth said as he tried to keep a straight face. "It appears our

guests have arrived. Children, you may be seated."

They hurried to find their seats . . . with their parents. Christi reached for her dad's hand. Becky hopped into Mr. McMercy's lap. The children looked nervously at their parents, who were no help at all. Their parents didn't smile. They didn't frown. They just sat there.

A few parents passed knowing glances while the children sat wide-eyed.

Pastor Alltruth thanked the students again for their testimonies. "I'd like to introduce to you now our special guest, Officer Goldtree. He is an undercover police officer, and he has something to share with the group tonight."

The officer pulled a crinkled newspaper out of his pocket. He stepped to the front, cleared his throat, and began reading.

Students "spring" surprise!

This summer students from Highland and Harmony Schools exchanged their sharp uniforms for work clothes and sweat, all for a wonderful goal. That goal was new computers for their schools. While other children slept late, these hard-working young people showed Godly character in overcoming challenges that would make many grown-ups quit.

That's not the end of the story, however. When a family needed help, the students decided, on their own, to give them the money from their biggest fund raiser, the Founders' Day bake sale. They never lost sight of their goal, even when their profits were stolen. The thief was caught and returned the money; so the story did have a happy ending. The Springer family were the ones who benefited from the students' generosity.

"I've never seen anyone like 'em," said Mr. Springer. "They really wanted to help us."

"They are my friends," said the oldest son, Bobby.

"They're the greatest," announced little Katie, jumping up and down in brand-new shoes. "Now Jesus is my best friend in the whole world."

"Nobody's ever done anything like this for us before," said Mrs. Springer.

Students "spring" surprise!

This summer students from Highland and Harmony Schools exchanged their sharp uniforms for work clothes and sweat, all for a wonderful goal. That goal was new computers for their schools. While other children slept late, these hard-working young people showed Godly character in overcoming challenges that would make many grown-ups quit.

That's not the end of the story, however. When a family needed help, the students decided, on their own, to give them the money from their biggest fundraiser, the Founder's Day bake sale. They never lost sight of their goal, even their profits stolen. The thief caught and returned money; so the did have a ending. The Spr family were the stu from the

Harold Gibson
guest writer
Highland Observer

who benefited from generosity.

"I've never seen anyone like Mr. Springer. "They really said th

They gave away nearly all their profits, but meeting the needs of others is more important to these students. In the words of Mayor Thotworthy, "Our community needs more young people with this kind of character."

You can help these unselfish young people still achieve their summer goal. Contact Highland or Harmony church offices or stop by The Fruit of the Spirit Bookstore on the square.

Hapford looked puzzled and then surprised; then a broad smile glowed on his face as the truth about everything that had happened that summer suddenly began to make sense. Parents stood up and clapped loudly.

"I think they knew before we did," whispered Ace to Pudge.

"I knew Mom was just too quiet on the way to the church tonight," Pudge said.

Questions bounced around in Christi's mind.

It's all perfectly clear now, reasoned Reginald. *The "criminal" wrote that article. He was the one who left the note about the money at the lemonade stand and hid that microphone under the red rag . . . er . . . scarf . . . er . . .*

"He's the one who took the pictures of Ronny stealing the money," gasped Miriam quietly.

"What's his name?" Booker nudged J. Michael.

"Children, meet Mr. Harold Gibson," Officer Goldtree said. "He's a guest writer for the *Highland Observer*. Here's his picture! He made the front page too!" The officer shifted his weight uncomfortably from one foot to the other as he remembered yesterday's questioning at the police station. "I'm sorry for the misunderstanding. You're certainly free to go now. I congratulate you on a job well done." The officer stepped back and reached for Mr. Gibson's hand. He wasn't handcuffed after all!

Pastor Gentle broke in. "And that's just the beginning. This morning, Pastor Alltruth and I have been flooded with calls from people offering to donate money for computers. They've already pledged

enough money for two computers and software!"

"He's not a criminal. He's a hero, just as I thought," Christi said under her breath. Mrs. Lovejoy hugged her.

"Let's go to the fellowship hall. I know you are all anxious to talk with Mr. Gibson," Pastor Alltruth said.

"Wow!" shouted Pudge as he surveyed the food and then the room. Sandwiches, cookies, and fruit dotted the front table of the hall. Balloons with long, curly ribbons waved at the end of each table. Streamers laced the doorways and a glittery banner pinned on the wall read, "Jesus is Lord!"

Mr. Gibson soaked it in. *God is good. He truly is good to those who follow Him.*

God had once again shown His hand, this time through Mr. Gibson and *The Red Rag Riddle.*